PAUL KRASSNER

Counterculture Hall of Fame, 2001 Inductee

Winner,
Playboy Award for satire
Feminist Party Media Workshop Award
for journalism

Oakland PEN Lifetime Achievement Award

"I told Krassner one time that his writings made me hopeful.
He found this an odd compliment to offer a satirist. I explained
that he made supposedly serious matters seem ridiculous, and
that this inspired many of his readers to decide for themselves
what was ridiculous and what was not. Knowing that there were
people doing that, better late than never, made me optimistic."
—Kurt Vonnegut

"The FBI was right; this man is dangerous.
And funny. And necessary."
—George Carlin

"He is an expert at ferreting out hypocrisy and absurdism
from the more solemn crannies of American culture."
—*New York Times*

"As soon as we de▮▮▮▮▮▮▮
Post, I knew I wa▮▮▮▮▮▮
irreverence was ju▮▮▮▮▮
—A▮▮▮

T0125664

PM PRESS OUTSPOKEN AUTHORS SERIES

PM PRESS OUTSPOKEN AUTHORS SERIES

Patty Hearst & The Twinkie Murders: A Tale of Two Trials

plus...

Patty Hearst & The Twinkie Murders: A Tale of Two Trials

plus

"Why Was Michelle Shocked Shell-Shocked?"

and

"Reflections of a Realist"
Outspoken Interview

Paul Krassner

PM PRESS | 2014

Portions of "The Trial of Patty Hearst" were published in the *Berkeley Barb* and *Playboy*. Portions of "The Case of the Twinkie Murders" were published in the *San Francisco Bay Guardian* and *The Nation*.

Patty Hearst & The Twinkie Murders: A Tale of Two Trials
Paul Krassner © 2014
This edition © 2014 PM Press

Series editor: Terry Bisson

ISBN: 978-1-62963-038-0
LCCN: 2014908068

Cover photo by Nancy Cain
Payphone by Alexander Graham Bell
Outsides: John Yates/Stealworks.com
Insides: Jonathan Rowland

PM Press
P.O. Box 23912
Oakland, CA 94623

10 9 8 7 6 5 4 3 2 1

Printed in the USA by the Employee Owners of Thomson-Shore in Dexter, Michigan
www.thomsonshore.com

CONTENTS

For Holly

"In the Halls of Justice, the only
justice is in the halls."
—Lenny Bruce

THE TRIAL OF PATTY HEARST

GROUCHO MARX SAID DURING an interview with *Flash* magazine in 1971, "I think the only hope this country has is Nixon's assassination." Yet he was not subsequently arrested for threatening the life of a president. In view of the indictment against Black Panther David Hilliard for using similar rhetoric, I wrote to the San Francisco office of the Justice Department to find out the status of their case against Groucho.

This was the response:

Dear Mr. Krassner:

Responding to your inquiry of July 7th, the United States Supreme Court has held that Title 18 U.S.C., section 871, prohibits only "true" threats. It is one thing to say that "I (or *we*) will kill Richard Nixon" when you are the leader of an organization which advocates killing people and overthrowing the

Government; it is quite another to utter the
words which are attributed to Mr. Marx, an
alleged comedian. It was the opinion of both
myself and the United States Attorney in Los
Angeles (where Marx's words were alleged to
have been uttered) that the latter utterance
did not constitute a "true" threat.

Very truly yours,
James L. Browning, Jr.
United States Attorney

Browning was so anxious in his pursuit of justice that
he successfully fought for the dismissal of charges against
federal narcotics officers who had shot an innocent hippie
in the back from their helicopter in Humboldt County. In
1976, I found myself sitting in a courtroom every day, ob-
serving Browning as he prosecuted a bank robbery case that
seemed like a perverted version of a Marx Brothers movie.

Patricia Hearst had been kidnapped by the Symbionese
Liberation Army—a group of white men and women led
by an African-American, Donald "Cinque" DeFreeze.
Patty was kept in a closet, then she joined them, changed
her name to Tania, adopted radical rhetoric and robbed a
bank with them. Now the philosophical paradox which
has plagued the history of human consciousness—*Is there
is or is there ain't Free Will?*—was finally going to be decided by a jury.

The abduction occurred in February 1974. One of
the SLA's demands was a free food program. Patty's father,
Randolph Hearst, publisher of the *San Francisco Examiner*,

arranged for such a project in Oakland. Then-governor Ronald Reagan responded to the long line of people waiting for free food: "I hope they all get botulism."

In June, I disclosed in the *Berkeley Barb* the non-fact that I had been brought to meet Patty underground. I wrote: "Since there is nothing of investigatory value in the interview, I will not speak with the FBI. Nor am I able to supply any information that might earn me a $50,000 reward. Tania insisted that she had not been brainwashed. My impression is that she was."

In view of conspiracy researcher Mae Brussell's track record with the Watergate story (titled "Why Was Martha Mitchell Kidnapped?"), I decided to devote an entire issue of *The Realist* to her documented analysis, "Why Was Patricia Hearst Kidnapped?"—the thrust of which was that the SLA was essentially an espionage plot orchestrated by our secret government in order to distort the message of idealism.

One year after the kidnapping, Patty Hearst was still on the lam with her captors, and *Crawdaddy*, a music magazine for which I wrote a column, "The Naked Emperor," wanted a feature article on the case. So I wrote an imaginary interview with Patty, and *Crawdaddy* published it in their April 1975 issue. An excerpt:

> **Q.** There was a pornographic novel, *Black Abductor*, published a couple of years ago, which seems to parallel your case on several counts, although in the book the kidnap victim is raped.
> **A.** That didn't happen to me. I wasn't raped, but I have made love—of my own free

will—with each and every one of my comrades. Male and female. And it's been extremely liberating. I'll tell you, I've learned more about my own sensuality in the past year than in my whole previous life.

Q. There's been a rumor that you used to visit Donald DeFreeze in prison?
A. That's impossible. It's a lie. I never did.

Q. And also that you knew [SLA member] Willie Wolfe before you were abducted?'
A. That's another lie. I mean, I feel as if I've known him all my life, but that's a false rumor.

Q. How have you been affected by the bisexuality?
A. I think it was an extension of heterosexuality. I had never been physically close to a black man like I've been with Cinque. I always thought nappy hair was tough—like Brillo, you know?—but it's really soft. And so then to become intimate with another woman—I could feel my inhibitions peeling off like layers of onion skin. And I became acquainted with my clitoris. My poor little neglected clitoris, ignored all these years. What a waste.

Q. What about the evidence that DeFreeze has been an informer for the Los Angeles Police Department?

A. That was his survival game. If he were still working for the pigs, we wouldn't be in danger now. I mean, you can't confuse somebody like Cinque with—like, I met the Shah of Iran once, and he was absolutely charming, but he's actually a vicious executioner. But I just hope that some of those Watergate bastards go to prison, just so they get even a little taste of it and perhaps understand the lengths that a prisoner will go to—the deals and all—to escape legally, if that's really legal.

Q. What about music? What have you been listening to?
A. Well, we only have a radio here. At a previous safe-house there was a stereo, but we didn't have a variety of records. Joy of Cooking, we played them a lot. Pink Floyd, too. And there's a group called the Last Poets, and there's one cut on their album where they give their interpretation of all the symbolism on a dollar bill, and we just sat around, wiped out on some really excellent grass, looking at a dollar bill while they were reciting that. It's very powerful. I remember how I used to think, when I was a little girl, that real money was just official play money.

Q. I feel silly asking this, but have you been brainwashed?

A. No, I've been *coerced*, obviously, at the beginning, but I haven't been brainwashed. You have to understand what it's been like from my point of view. Instant introspection. The moment I was taken away, underneath the tremendous fear I felt, I was still aware that it was because I was the daughter of a wealthy family whose comfort depends on the suffering of others. I've always been vaguely aware of that but, you know, you try to repress that kind of thing so you can go on living comfortably yourself.

Q. Did your family know you were getting stoned?
A. Oh, sure. Listen, there was almost a pound of marijuana at our apartment when I, you know, went on this little involuntary vacation trip, but I'll bet my father and the FBI made some kind of agreement to keep it quiet. They couldn't very well pretend that Steven smoked and I didn't.

Q. You were real close to Steven Weed. How do you view that relationship now?
A. It seems like a previous incarnation. He had been my math teacher at Crystal Springs, but I was the aggressive one. In fact, that made me have sort of a vested interest in him—like he was an emotional *investment*, you know? And there was something, an

adolescent romantic fantasy, about making out with your *tutor*. You got status for being independent.

But we ended up leading a very middle-class life in Berkeley. Listening to records, dinner parties—always with *his* friends, couples—and shopping for antiques, that was fun. But it was like a couple of children playing house, with my father helping out—with an MG here, and a $1,500 Persian rug there—Dad was saving *that* for a wedding present. *God!*

Sex was okay with us, but not really anything passionate. The only affection I got was foreplay. It was always a means to an end. It was always *functional*.

Q. You said on one of the communiqués that the FBI wants you dead. Why is that?

A. Because I *know* too much, obviously. It's not just the FBI, but also my father's corporation advisors. I remember the way I used to hate hippies—who were in my own *age* bracket. I had to justify that hatred by bringing in the puritan ethic. Hippies were unproductive, right?

Anybody who cooperates with the FBI is signing their own death warrant. And it's the same with the pig corporate structure. Their whole existence is devoted to perverting innocent children into consumers.

Why do you think my mother wanted me to go to Stanford instead of Berkeley even though she's a goddamn *regent* for the University? What kind of hypocrisy is *that?* She helps control a school that's not good enough for her own *daughter* to go to?

Well, *I'm* a hippie now. *I'm* a white nigger now.

Q. What exactly is it that you know too much about?

A. Well, that my whole kidnapping was *scripted* by the government . . .

● ● ●

Earth News Service had called the FBI in San Francisco to find out why they didn't investigate me when I originally announced in the *Barb* that I had met with Patty Hearst in captivity. An agent checked the files and found a notation that I had also announced that I would never cooperate with the FBI, so they didn't bother. However, a week after *Crawdaddy* came out, a pair of FBI agents from the Santa Cruz office visited me at my home in Watsonville, wanting to talk about the interview.

"I'm sorry," I said, opening the door a crack, "but I have nothing to tell you."

They repeated their request, still friendly and low-key.

"Everything I had to say about that has already been published," I explained. "There's nothing further to discuss."

They tried to peer in my window.

"Patty isn't here, is she?"

"If you get a search warrant, I'll let you look."

In the middle of a *Doonesbury* strip, Garry Trudeau spelled out the word Canaan, which was the city where a friend of his lived, but federal authorities were convinced it was really a reference to Patty Hearst's supposed hideout in Pennsylvania.

William F. Buckley wrote that Patty should be sacrificed "in the name of Christ." And Catherine Hearst said that she would rather her daughter be dead than join the Communists. She also commented that if only Clark Gable had been at the apartment in Berkeley instead of Steven Weed, then Patty would never have been kidnapped.

Probably true.

• • •

Patty Hearst was finally captured after eighteen months. Although her own cousin Will said that he would not have recognized her, the arresting officer immediately said, "Patty, what are *you* doing here?" She was so surprised that she peed in her pants, an accident acknowledged in the *Chronicle*, but not in the *Examiner*. She was permitted to change in the bathroom.

The FBI inventory did not include "pants, wet, one pair," but there was on their list "a two-foot marijuana plant"—as compared with almost a *pound* of pot that was *not* reported by the FBI that was found at the apartment from which she had originally been kidnapped. There was also a bottle of Gallo wine in the SLA safe-house—not exactly a loyal gesture to the grape boycott of the United Farm Workers, whom they purported to support. And there was an unidentified "rock" found in Patty's purse.

A KGO newscaster reported breathlessly: "Patti Page has been captured!"

• • •

I had a lunch appointment with Will Hearst, assistant to the editor at the *Examiner* and grandson of Citizen Kane's prototype, William Randolph Hearst. Although Will claimed that his status as Patty's favorite cousin was a media creation, he was the very first one she requested to see after her arrest. Now he walked into the *Examiner* lobby.

"It's a bad day," he told me. "San Simeon has been bombed."

"Well," I said, "at least I have an alibi."

We postponed the lunch, and on the way home I stopped at the federal court building, where Patty's trial was in a preliminary stage. Originally, she was going to be defended by the radical team of Vincent Hallinan and his son, Kayo. The elder Hallinan was in Honolulu when the FBI captured Patty, so he assigned Kayo to visit her in jail. Although as Tania she had called Vincent Hallinan a "clown" in a taped communiqué, now, as Patty, she said of Kayo, "He's good. Like, I really trust him politically and personally, and I can tell him just about anything I want and he's cool." It was, however, a lawyer-client relationship that would not be permitted to mature.

When Patty described her physical reaction to having her blindfold removed in captivity, Kayo recognized a similarity to reactions to LSD. Patty agreed that there had been something reminiscent of her acid trips with Steven Weed in the old Hearst mansion.

Besides, there was circumstantial evidence that the SLA could have dosed her with LSD: the brother of SLA member Mizmoon reported that she and fellow member Camilla Hall had taken acid; in *TV Guide*, reporter Marilyn Baker claimed that drugs had been found at the SLA safe-house in Concord; and on the very first taped communiqué, Patty herself had said, "I caught a cold, but they're giving me pills for it and stuff."

Her defense was going to be involuntary intoxication, a side effect of which is amnesia. So Patty would neither have to snitch on others nor invoke the Fifth Amendment for her own protection. In response to any questions about that missing chunk of her life, she was simply going to assert, "I have no recollection." The Hallinans instructed her not to talk to anybody—especially psychiatrists—about that period.

But her uncle, William Randolph Hearst, Jr., editor-in-chief of the Hearst newspaper chain, flew in from the East Coast to warn his family that the entire corporate image of the Hearst empire was at stake, and they'd better hire an establishment attorney—fast. Enter F. Lee Bailey. He had defended a serial killer (the Boston Strangler) and a war criminal (Captain Harold Medina of My Lai massacre infamy), but he said he would not defend Patty Hearst if she were a revolutionary. You've got to have standards.

Bailey and his partner, Albert Johnson, visited with Patty for a couple of hours at San Mateo County Jail in order to encourage her to tell the psychiatrists *everything* and *not* say, "I have no recollection." She could trust these doctors, they assured her, and nothing she said could be used against her in any way. Now her defense would be based on the Stockholm Hostage Syndrome. Patty had been kidnapped again.

Brainwashing does exist. Built into the process is the certainty that one has not been brainwashed. Patty's obedience to her defense team paralleled her obedience to the SLA. The survival syndrome had simply changed hands. F. Lee Bailey was Cinque in whiteface. Instead of a machine-gun, he owned a helicopter company—Enstrom, an anagram for Monster. Instead of taping underground communiqués, he held press conferences. It was all show biz.

There had been a rumor that Patty was pregnant by Cinque. Indeed, one of the first questions that Randolph Hearst asked when he met sports figure Jack Scott—who had supposedly seen Patty on the lam—was to ascertain if that rumor was true. I wrote in the *Berkeley Barb:* "Now, with their daughter on trial, the Hearsts have hired a lawyer who wears pancake make-up to press conferences, the better to transform a racist fear into a Caucasian alibi."

I received this letter by certified mail:

Dear Sir:

You undoubtedly did not realize that the name "Pan-Cake Make-Up is the registered trademark (U.S. Patent Office No. 350,402) of Max Factor & Co., and is not a synonym for cake make-up. The correct usage is "Pan-Cake Make-Up", capitalized and written in just that manner, or, under circumstances such as these, where you obviously did not intend to mention a particular brand, simply cake make-up.

We are sure that you are aware of the legal importance of protecting a trademark and trust that you will use ours properly in any future reference to our product, or, in the alternative, will use the proper generic term rather than our brand name. So that our records will be complete, we would appreciate an acknowledgment of this letter.

Very truly yours,
Max Factor & Co.
D. James Pekin
Corporate Counsel

In response, l explained that there had been "a slight misunderstanding—what F. Lee Bailey had been wearing to all those press conferences was actually Aunt Jemima Pancake Mix—and I hope that has cleared up the matter."

• • •

It was not an easy task for *Examiner* reporter Stephen Cook to report about the trial of his boss's daughter, what with the boss sitting right there in the front row of the courtroom to oversee him, but he didn't spare his employer from embarrassing testimony; and, to the *Examiner's* credit, he was not censored. However, Dick Alexander, who was writing feature material on the trial for the *Examiner*, had his copy changed so drastically that he requested his byline be dropped.

On the first day of the trial, he wore a tie with the legendary *Fuck You* emblazoning the design. Randolph Hearst chastised him for this, but Alexander continued to wear the tie. Perhaps it reminded Hearst of the time Patty screamed, "Fuck you, Daddy!" in his office. A syndicated cartoon by George Lichty—with the caption, "I don't know whether she was brainwashed, but she should certainly have her mouth washed out with soap!"—appeared only in the first edition of the *Examiner*.

The trial was also grist for the TV entertainment mill. On *The Merv Griffin Show*, the audience voted 70–30 that Patty was guilty as charged. On the sitcom *Maude*, the British maid studying for her citizenship test had to answer the question, "Who said, 'Give me liberty or give me death'?" She was given a hint that the initials were P.H. She did not guess Patrick Henry, but Patty Hearst. And Johnny Carson in his opening monologue wondered whether F. Lee Bailey would get Lockheed off "for kidnapping our money."

Soap-opera actress Ruth Warrick, who starred in *Citizen Kane*, revealed that "My name was not printed in any Hearst paper for five years after that film was released. I could be the star of a movie and my name couldn't even be mentioned in the ads in Hearst papers."

Patty had never seen *Citizen Kane*, particularly not while on the run, because it would've been too embarrassing to be caught with it. Throughout her trial, there was a screen set up in the court, but instead of Orson Welles, over and over and over again, like some recurring nightmare, Patty would view footage of herself helping to rob the Hibernia Bank. One witness at the bank had been convinced that it was merely an episode for the TV series, *Streets of San Francisco*, and that Patty was just an actress.

Nancy Faber of *People* magazine became the unofficial courtroom fashion advisor. If you wanted to find out exactly what color Patty's pantsuit was, Faber would know that it was Iranian Rust. But while Patty was wearing light-brown eye shadow, or pearl-gray nail polish to indicate that she didn't have the hands of a criminal, the San Quentin Six were appearing before *their* jury each day in shackles and leg irons. Shana Alexander was the only journalist who skipped a day at the Patty Hearst trial to attend the San Quentin Six trial.

A rhetorical question had been asked of the press: "How can you justify extensive coverage of Patty Hearst and say little, if anything, about the San Quentin Six, in which the state has admitted not having any real evidence?" KQED interviewed media folks, who rationalized that they were only giving the public what it wanted.

But when you had a TV program like *Mowgli's Brothers*, an animated cartoon based on Rudyard Kipling's *Jungle Books*, in which an abandoned baby is adopted by a couple of compassionate wolves who talk to him—and right there in the middle there's a commercial with Tony the Tiger telling young viewers that they should eat Frosted Flakes—was that not a form of brainwashing? The San Quentin Six were to Patty Hearst as ginseng root was to Frosted Flakes.

John Lester of KPIX became the media advisor for the Hearst family when Patty was abducted. He warned Randolph Hearst that when he stepped through his front door he would be appearing on international television and therefore it would be important not to pick his nose. So, just before he opened the door, Hearst would call out, "Hey, John—look!"

Lester would look, and Hearst would proceed to stick his index finger up his right nostril, eliciting a horrified laugh from his media advisor. Then Hearst would walk out with Catherine wearing a black dress and mournfully greet the press. On the inside of the door, there was a sign that warned "Don't Pick Your Nose!"

Patty's parents were there on view when the jury was selected, although the press was excluded. But how could the judge be sure that Randolph Hearst wouldn't leak the story to his own paper? And so they sat in the front row of the courtroom each day, that protective image of media royalty continuing to lurk behind Princess Patty in the subconscious memory of the jurors.

What was really on trial was this royal nuclear family—the floor sample of a consumer unit that also served as the original source of authority. If Patty had not "belonged" to her parents, why would anybody want to kidnap her? And if the princess had lived her pre-kidnap life inside the safety of a castle, then how could any nasty old SLA manage to get her?

The message of this trial was clear: Destroy the seeds of rebellion in your children or we shall have it done *for* you. In the courtroom, spectators with binoculars focused on Patty and her parents, who were busy pretending that they weren't being watched for reactions. They had become a captive audience by being forced to listen in public to a tape-recorded communiqué from their princess, abdicating her right to the throne:

Mom, Dad, I would like to comment on your efforts to supposedly secure my safety. The [food] giveaway was a sham . . . You were playing games—stalling for time—which the FBI was using in their attempts to assassinate me and the SLA elements which guarded me . . .

I have been given the choice of, one, being released in a safe area or, two, joining the forces of the Symbionese Liberation Army . . . I have chosen to stay and fight . . .

I want you to tell the people the truth. Tell them how the law-and-order programs are just a means to remove so-called violent— meaning *aware*—individuals from the community in order to facilitate the controlled removal of unneeded labor forces in this country, in the same way that Hitler controlled the removal of the Jews from Germany.

I should have known that if you and the rest of the corporate state were willing to do this to millions of people to maintain power and to serve your needs, you would also kill me if necessary to serve those same needs. How long will it take before white people in this country understand that whatever happens to a black child happens sooner or later to a white child? How long will it be before we all understand that we must fight for our freedom?

At the end of the tape, Donald "Cinque" DeFreeze came on with a triple death threat, especially to one Colston

Westbrook, whom he accused of being "a government agent now working for military intelligence while giving assistance to the FBI." This communiqué was originally sent to San Francisco radio station KSAN. News director David McQueen checked with a Justice Department source, who confirmed Westbrook's employment by the CIA.

Conspiracy researcher Mae Brussell traced Westbrook's activities from 1962, when he was a CIA advisor to the South Korean CIA, through 1969, when he provided logistical support in Vietnam for the CIA's Phoenix program. His job was the indoctrination of assassination and terrorist cadres.

After seven years in Asia, he was brought home in 1970, along with the war, and assigned to run the Black Cultural Association at Vacaville Prison, where he became the control officer for DeFreeze, who had worked as a police informer from 1967 to 1969 for the Public Disorder Intelligence Unit of the Los Angeles Police Department.

If DeFreeze was a double agent, then the SLA was a Frankenstein monster, turning against its creator by becoming in reality what had been orchestrated only as a media image. When he snitched on his keepers, he signed the death warrant of the SLA. They were burned alive in a Los Angeles safe-house during a shootout with police. When Cinque's charred remains were sent to his family in Cleveland, they couldn't help but notice that he had been decapitated. It was as if the CIA had said, literally, "Bring me the head of Donald DeFreeze!"

Consider the revelations of Wayne Lewis in August 1975. He claimed to have been an undercover agent for the FBI, a fact verified by FBI director Clarence Kelley. Surfacing at a press conference in Los Angeles, Lewis spewed forth a veritable conveyor belt of conspiratorial charges: that DeFreeze was an FBI informer; that he was killed not by the SWAT team but by an FBI agent because he had become "uncontrollable"; that the FBI then wanted Lewis to infiltrate the SLA; that the FBI had undercover agents in other underground guerrilla groups; that the FBI knew where Patty Hearst was but let her remain free so it could build up its files of potential subversives.

At one point, the FBI declared itself to have made 27,000 checks into the whereabouts of Patty Hearst. It was simultaneously proclaimed by the FDA that there were 25,000 brands of laxative on the market. That meant one catharsis for each FBI investigation, with a couple of thousand potential loose shits remaining to smear across "No Left Turn" signs. Patty had become a vehicle for repressive action on the right and for wishful thinking on the left.

• • •

A three-month-old baby, whose mother wanted to expose her to the process of justice, was being breast-fed in the back of the courtroom while Patty Hearst testified that she had been raped in a closet by the lover she had once described as "the gentlest, most beautiful man I've ever known."

Now, prosecutor James Browning was cross-examining her.

"Did you, in fact, have a strong feeling for Willie Wolfe?"

"In a way, yes."

"As a matter of fact, were you in love with him?"

"No."

A little later, Browning asked if it had been "forcible rape."

"Excuse me?

"Did you struggle or submit?"

"I didn't resist. I was afraid."

Browning walked into the trap: "I thought you said you had strong feelings for him?"

"I did," Patty replied triumphantly. "I couldn't *stand* him."

It sure seemed fake. Yet there was this letter-to-the-editor of the *Berkeley Barb*:

> Only a woman knows that the sex act, no matter how gentle, becomes rape if she is an unwilling partner. Her soul, as well as her body, is scarred. The gentleness of Willie Wolfe does not preclude rape. Rape, in this instance, was dependent upon Patricia Hearst's state of mind, not Willie Wolfe's. We must all remember that *only* Patty knows what *she* felt; and if we refuse to believe her, there can be no justice.

Patty also said that her intercourse with Cinque was "without affection."

The SLA women insisted they were not "mindless cunts enslaved by big black penises."

"You need seven inches," a reporter was explaining, "for a byline in *Newsweek*."

"Patty Frigid After DeFreeze," stated a headline that was set in type but not used in the *Daily Californian*, the Berkeley campus newspaper.

"Hearst Blows Weed," stated a later headline that *was* used in the *Daily Californian*.

"Is the government saying," objected F. Lee Bailey, "that everyone who smokes grass is a bank robber?"

Oh, that's right, this *was* a bank-robbery trial, wasn't it?

"Were you *acting* the part of a bank robber?" Browning asked Patty.

"I was doing exactly what I had to do. I just wanted to get *out* of that bank. I was just supposed to be in there to get my picture taken, mostly."

Ulysses Hall testified that after the robbery, he managed to speak on the phone with his former prison mate, Cinque, who told him that the SLA members didn't trust Patty's decision to join them. Conversely, *she* didn't trust *their* offer of a "choice," since they all realized that she'd be able to identify them if she went free—and so they made her prove herself by "fronting her off" at the bank with Cinque's gun pointed at her head. Out of the closet, into the bank!

Patty testified that Patricia Soltysik kicked her because she wasn't enthusiastic enough at a dress rehearsal, and that Cinque warned her that if she messed up in any way, she'd be killed. Before the trial, prosecutor Browning had admitted that it was "clear from the photographs she may have been acting under duress." And during the trial, Bailey, with only fifteen minutes to go before weekend recess, brought out the government's suppression of photos showing Camilla Hall also pointing her gun at Patty in the bank.

Moreover, in a scene right out of *Blow-Up* or an aspirin commercial, a "scientific laboratory" had used a digital computer "to filter out the grain without changing the content," then scanned the photos with a laser beam, all to indicate that Patty had opened her mouth in surprise and recoiled in horror at the firing of shots in the bank, and that it was merely a shadow that made her look as if she were smiling during the robbery, although Cinque had given her strict orders to smile whenever she met anyone who was supposed to know she was Tania, because the original image of Patty, the one that was disseminated around the world, showed her smiling broadly.

No wonder KQED's courtroom artist Rosalie Ritz was approached by a promoter willing to pay her to design a Patty doll with a complete change of clothes so it could be turned into a Tania doll.

It did not come out in the testimony of Louis "Jolly" West that he had once killed an elephant with an overdose of LSD—which United Press correspondent Don Thackrey called "Pachydermicide"—nor that Dr. West had once spent eight straight hours in John Lilly's sensory deprivation tank.

According to Kayo Hallinan, Patty "hated" West because she was aware of the fascistic implications of his proposed UCLA Center for the Study and Reduction of Violence, which would practice what it preached against—violence—in the form of electrode implantation and aversion therapy. Obviously, then, some kind of coercive persuasion must have been used to get her to talk to him. Perhaps she had been reduced to a state of infantile helplessness—once again.

A letter from a prisoner in the San Mateo Jail:

I was coming out of the doctor's office when I saw Tania being taken out the front door. The guards had cleared the hallways of all prisoners and it was by mistake that I was let out at that time by the jail nurse. Tania was taken out by one female and three males. When I called to her I was dragged out of the hallway. Our comrade was exhausted and frightened, lethargic in her movements and appeared drugged. While I was in the doctor's office, I had noticed a 3-by-5 manila envelope—the type used to hold medications given to prisoners—which had written on it, "Hearst." There is little doubt she is being drugged.

The Associated Press reported that "a source close to the specialists conducting the examination . . . said that the dosages of 'anti-psychotic drugs' listed on Miss Hearst's medical report would themselves cause lethargy and disorientation." Would she eventually emerge from the psychiatric kidnapping only to proclaim, as she had previously done on an SLA communiqué, "I have not been brainwashed, drugged, tortured or hypnotized in any way"?

F. Lee Bailey put Patty on the witness stand. He asked her what Cinque had done on one occasion to show his disapproval.

"He pinched me."

"Where?"

"My breasts"—pause—"and down—"

"Your private parts as well?"

"Yes."

Then Browning cross-examined Patty:

"Did he pinch one or both of your breasts?"

"I really don't remember."

"Was it under your clothing?"

"Yes."

"In both places?"

"Pardon me, I don't think that the other was under my clothing."

"All right, your breasts he pinched by touching your skin. The pubic area, he didn't touch your skin. Is that true?"

"That's right."

Good Lord, this was supposed to be the Trial of the Century, and the government was busy trying to find out whether Cinque got bare tit.

Bailey fought unsuccessfully to have Patty testify about the bombing of the Hearst castle, so that the jury would know she was still, indirectly, afraid of SLA members Bill and Emily Harris. But, once more, Patty tricked Browning during cross-examination. He was asking why she hadn't taken advantage of opportunities to phone for help.

"It wasn't possible for me to call," she explained, "because I couldn't do it, and I was afraid of the FBI."

Browning was certainly not going to disagree with Bailey's contention that Patty suffered from "a misperception about the viciousness of the FBI," so he asked Patty if it had occurred to her to turn the Harrises in.

"I was afraid. They aren't the only people like that running around . . . There were many others who could've picked up right where they left off."

Browning wondered if they really had such "power over your life."

THE TRIAL OF PATTY HEARST | 25

"They did. It's happening right now."

"Has somebody been killed?"

Suddenly, Patty switched from her usual monotone to a hurried delineation of the latest terrorist acts, threats, and broken promises, including this: "San Simeon was bombed. My parents received a communiqué demanding $250,000—"

Your Honor, please, the witness is leading the prosecutor. But it was too late. The jury had heard her.

Browning countered weakly: "Was anybody killed?"

"No."

• • •

Before the trial, Bailey's associate, Albert Johnson, had protested that, "contrary to what Sheriff McDonald says, [Patty Hearst and Sara Jane Moore, attempted assassin of President Ford] have not exchanged cordialities . . . I don't want any inferences drawn from any conduct of the two of them simply because they are in the same institution, because there is absolutely no connection between the two cases."

But there *was* a missing link—the murder of Wilbert "Popeye" Jackson, leader of the United Prisoners Union. He had been killed, together with a companion, Sally Voye, while they sat in a parked car at two o'clock in the morning. I learned from impeccable sources that the hit *was known in advance* within the California Department of Corrections, the FBI, and the San Jose and San Francisco police departments. But now—in mid-February 1976, while the Patty Hearst trial was still in process—a similar charge was made in the company of some unusual accusations when a Berkeley underground group called Tribal Thumb prepared this statement:

> It has become known to the Tribal Thumb orbit that the CIA, FBI and CCS [Criminal Conspiracy Section] have made undercurrent moves to establish a basis for the total eradication of the Tribal Thumb Community. . . . [They] are involved in working overtime to unravel the mystery of Popeye Jackson's execution in an effort to plant Tribal Thumb in a web of conspiracy in that execution . . .
>
> The FBI's heavy involvement in the case of Popeye's death largely is due to the death of Sally Voye, who in actuality was moonlighting (outside her employment as a teacher) as a narcotics agent for police forces. Moreover, she was Popeye's control agent. Popeye was an informer on the movement.
>
> Several days ago, Patty Hearst was slipped out of her jail cell by the FBI and Mr. Randolph Hearst and taken to a nearby jail to identify a man being held there (we're withholding his name for now) who was allegedly closely associated with Tribal Thumb, to make an identification of this man's alleged trafficking of large quantities of arms to Tribal Thumb and the Symbionese Liberation Army. The result is that Miss Hearst pointed the comrade out as the trafficker of such weapons . . .

Donald DeFreeze escaped from the California prison system with help from the FBI and California prison officials. His mission was to establish an armed revolutionary organization, controlled by the FBI, specifically to either make contact with or undermine the surfacing and development of the August Seventh Guerrilla Movement [ASGM].

We make note of the fact that the first communiqué issued by the SLA under the leadership of Donald DeFreeze was in part a duplicate of a communiqué issued by the ASGM. Further examination of those communiqués establishes that the ASGM had surfaced and was in the process of developing some kind of operational format, when the SLA hastily moved, hard pressed for something spectacular to cut off this thrust by the ASGM. The result was the incorrect and unfounded death of (school superintendent) Marcus Foster.

It is evident that the FBI through its sources of information knew of the underground existence of the ASGM and that the movement was obviously making plans to become public knowledge via armed actions against the imperialist state. Having had their attempts to infiltrate agents into the ASGM's mainstream frustrated, they sought the diverse method of establishing an organization they could control. So they made three approaches: Donald DeFreeze, who was in contact with Nancy Ling Perry, who worked at Rudy's Fruit Stand, from whom Patty Hearst often bought bagels and fruit juice.

DeFreeze was let loose and given a safe plan to surface as an armed guerrilla unit. That plan was to kidnap Patty Hearst—strategized by the FBI, Randolph Hearst, Patty Hearst and Nancy Ling Perry. The format of that plan of kidnapping Patty Hearst was extracted from a book, published by a publishing company named Nova, owned by the Hearst Corporation, titled *Vanished*.

On April 8, after Patty was found guilty, there was a front-page story in the *San Francisco Examiner*:

Would-be presidential assassin Sara Jane Moore and the Patricia Hearst case are intricately linked in the web of evidence that led to yesterday's arrest of the accused murderer of militant prison-reform leader Wilbert "Popeye" Jackson, authorities have told the *Examiner*.

These sources said Ms. Moore, now in custody in a Federal prison in San Diego, will be a star witness in the trial of the accused slayer . . . And it was the arrest last September of Miss Hearst . . . that led to the break in the case, according to the primary investigators in the case . . .

> Booked into the San Francisco County Jail yesterday afternoon was Richard Alan London 26, an ex-convict who has been in the Santa Clara County Jail in San Jose since last summer on an armed-robbery charge . . . London is a member of a revolutionary band called the United Prisoners Union . . .
>
> Federal and local authorities flatly denied a report circulated by Tribal Thumb sources that Miss Hearst, convicted of bank robbery on March 20, was taken to the Santa Clara jail to identify London last week . . .

Last week? Why this change in chronology? The original Tribal Thumb statement alleged that Patty had identified London as a gunrunner for the SLA and Tribal Thumb more than a *month-and-a-half* previously. The truth is that she secretly began to turn state's evidence *early in her trial.* Usually, defendants tell what they know *before* trial, so the prosecution can decide whether or not to plea-bargain and avoid a trial.

But this particular trial *had* to be held, if only to avoid giving any impression of plea-bargaining. Patty Hearst had been gang-banged behind the tent at the Hearstling Brothers Browning & Bailey Bread and Circus by both teams, prosecution and defense, while they were adversaries in a trial that was more carefully staged than a TV wrestling match.

Judge Oliver Carter had once sentenced Hedy Sarney to two and a half years for bank robbery. She claimed at her sentencing that Tribal Thumb had made her do it.

Now F. Lee Bailey reminded the judge that he had commented that her claim of coercion came too late and that she had refused to testify against the people she accused of forcing her to commit the crime, whereas, in the case of Patty Hearst, Bailey said cryptically, "Your Honor has been made aware of some facts which are relevant to him."

• • •

It was considered likely that Popeye Jackson could have been killed by police agents—to neutralize yet another black leader, rather than because he was supposed to be an informer. The United Prisoners Union reasoned that "if Popeye had been interested in snitching, he would have made all efforts to keep up his contacts with the NWLF (New World Liberation Front) rather than be 'cold and distant' or allow for any misunderstanding."

But was it possible, as Tribal Thumb pointed out, that Patty Hearst had participated in the planning of her own kidnapping while ostensibly *buying bagels?* An SLA manuscript stated that they had expected more trouble from their intended victim, "since we were planning on carrying her away, but she turned out to be real cooperative. She just lay down on the floor while one of the comrades tied her hands and blindfolded her."

When Patty was being interviewed in jail by prosecution psychiatrist Harry Kozol, it was as if she pulled a Raskolnikov (the character in Dostoyevsky's *Crime and Punishment* who cannot repress the force of his own guilt) by darting from the room and complaining that Kozol had accused her of arranging her own kidnapping.

Bailey asked him on the witness stand, "Did you suggest that she got herself kidnapped?"

"No."

In their first session, Kozol questioned Patty about Willie Wolfe.

"I told her," he testified, "that I'd heard her speak tenderly of him [on the final taped communiqué], and I asked her this question: 'Is that the way you felt about him?' She seemed to get upset and deeply moved. I felt she was almost sobbing inside . . . but no tears ran down her face. . . . She said, 'I don't *know* how I feel about him.' I said, 'I'm not asking you how you feel. Is that how you *felt*?' She became very much upset, began to shake and quiver, obviously suffering. And she answered, 'I don't know why I got into this goddamn thing—shit!' And then got up and left the room, terribly upset."

Got into *what* goddamn thing? Patty could have been referring to her agreement to talk with psychiatrists, or to her decision to join the SLA, or the kidnapping itself. In their second session, when she described the kidnapping scene, Kozol asked if there was anything else. He testified:

> There was some delay. She was sort of thinking. She began to look very uncomfortable, and I told her, "Never mind." And she said, "I don't want to tell you." And I said, "That's okay, if it makes you uncomfortable," and then she blurted out that she was going to tell me anyway. She told me that four days before the kidnapping, while she was sitting in class,

she was suddenly struck with a terrible fear that she was going to be kidnapped.

This was an overwhelming sensation. It stayed with her. I said, "What's so surprising about a girl from a well-to-do family worrying about kidnapping?" She brushed it aside and said, "It wasn't anything of the sort. It was different." For four solid days, she couldn't shake the fear. She finally thought in terror of running home to her parents, where she would be safe. She somehow fought that. Then the thing she dreaded, occurred.

•••

The family of slain SLA member Willie Wolfe hired Lake Headley—an ex-police intelligence officer who was chief investigator at Wounded Knee—to find out what had really happened. What he discovered, with fellow researchers Donald Freed and Rusty Rhodes, was that the SLA was part of the CIA's CHAOS program. In that context, they were planning to kill Black Panther leader Huey Newton and succeeded in killing black school superintendent Marcus Foster *after* he agreed to meet Panther demands for educational reforms.

At Vacaville Prison, DeFreeze was permitted to set up Unisight, a program by which convicts could get laid by visiting females. According to investigator Headley, DeFreeze's visitors included kidnappers-to-be Nancy Ling Perry and Patricia Soltysik—*and* Patty Hearst, then eighteen, not going under her own name but using the ID of Mary Alice Siems, a student at Berkeley.

Headley's affidavit stated: "That Patricia Campbell Hearst and her parents disagreed bitterly over Patricia's political and personal relations. That a love affair between a black man and Patricia Hearst did take place prior to her relationship with her fiancé Steven Weed. That Mrs. Randolph A. Hearst subjected her daughter to extreme pressure to change her personal and political relationships."

Patty began living with Weed in Berkeley later that year, in the fall of 1972. DeFreeze was transferred to Soledad Prison in December 1972, where he was given the special privilege of using the trailers ordinarily reserved for married trustees. DeFreeze became a leader of the SLA and, according to Headley, renewed his affair with Patty for a brief time. The affidavit continued: "Discussions were held between Patricia Campbell Hearst and the Symbionese Liberation Army concerning a kidnapping— not her own."

Whose, then? Her sisters, Anne and Vicki. The idea of kidnapping Patty, too, was brought up—this was a year before it actually took place—but she didn't think it was such a great option. However, if true, this would explain Patty's outburst at the moment of kidnapping: "Oh, no! Not *me!* Oh, God! Please let me go!" Not to mention her confession of pre-kidnap fear to Dr. Kozol.

The investigators presented their findings to the Los Angeles City Council, charging that the intelligence unit of the police department—the Criminal Conspiracy Section—knew of the SLA's presence but *wanted* the shootout for test purposes. Headley acquired official film footage of the massacre, showing that the FBI used a pair of German Shepherds to sniff out Patty's presence and make sure she wouldn't be inside the safe-house.

Steven Weed was told by a cop at the shootout, "Don't worry, Patty's not in there."

On the tape of April 3, 1974, Patty said, "I have been given the name Tania after a comrade who fought alongside Che in Bolivia for the people." And on tape of June 6, she said, "I renounced my class privilege when Cin [DeFreeze] and Cujo [Willie Wolfe] gave me the name Tania." But in a *New Times* interview, Bill Harris said, "She chose the name Tania herself."

According to Weed, her reading matter had ranged from the Marquis de Sade to *Do It* by Jerry Rubin. And, according to my Berkeley source, Patty and a former roommate had both read the book *Tania, the Unforgettable Guerrilla* a year prior to the kidnapping.

Further, I was told, the roommate had been subpoenaed to testify for the prosecution in Patty's trial, but the subpoena was withdrawn. I wrote about that in the *Berkeley Barb*. The FBI's liaison to the U.S. Attorney's office, Parks Stearns Jr., denied this vehemently, shouting at me in the press room, "You're wrong!"

It could've been just a coincidence, but after that incident, the head marshal began hassling me for identification, even though I had been coming to the trial every day. One time he asked for my driver's license. I told him I didn't drive a car. Another time he asked for my Social Security card. I told him I never carried that around. I would present only my press credentials, which he accepted because there were too many media people around, and he didn't want the attention that a scene would automatically create.

• • •

While Patty's trial was in progress, *Sundaz*, a Santa Cruz weekly, reported that Research West—the private right-wing spy organization that maintained files supplied by confessed burglar Jerome Ducote—"was purchased in October of 1969 with funds provided by Catherine Hearst," and that "after the Hearst connection became known to employees . . . at least one *Examiner* reporter was told to drop any further investigation into the Ducote case."

The *Sundaz* story stated not only that Catherine Hearst gave or lent most of the $60,000–$70,000 purchase price for the company, but also that prior to the purchase, the foundation supported itself through "contributions" averaging $1,000, provided by Pacific Telephone, Pacific Gas & Electric, railroads, steamship lines, banks and the *Examiner*. In return, the files were available to those companies, as well as to local police and sheriff departments, the FBI, the CIA and the IRS. The *Examiner* paid $1,500 a year through 1975 to retain the services of Research West.

In another case, a member of the Santa Clara district attorney's office testified that FBI agent Charles Bates had "categorically denied" having any of the stolen documents sought by the Santa Clara district attorney for an investigation of FBI-sponsored political burglaries. After being confronted with the testimony of one of his own subordinates, Bates ultimately turned over the documents. Some of the stolen documents, according to *Sundaz*, ended up with Catherine Hearst's pet project, Research West.

In 1969, Charles Bates was a Special Agent at the Chicago office of the FBI when police killed Black Panthers Fred Hampton and Mark Clark while they were sleeping. Ex-FBI informer Maria Fischer told the *Chicago Daily News* that the then-chief of the FBI's Chicago office, Marlon Johnson, personally asked her to slip a drug to Hampton; she had infiltrated the Black Panther Party at the FBI's request a month before. The drug was a tasteless, colorless liquid that would put him to sleep. She refused. Hampton was killed a week later. An autopsy showed "a near fatal dose" of secobarbital in his system.

In 1971, Bates was transferred to Washington, DC. According to Watergate burglar James McCord's book, *A Piece of Tape*, on June 21, 1972 (four days after the break-in), White House attorney John Dean checked with acting FBI Director L. Patrick Gray as to who was in charge of handling the Watergate investigation. The answer: Charles Bates—the same FBI official who in 1974 would be in charge of handling the SLA investigation and the search for Patty Hearst. When she was arrested, Bates became instantly ubiquitous on radio and TV, boasting of her capture.

And, in the middle of her trial—on a Saturday afternoon, when reporters and technicians were hoping to be off duty—the FBI called a press conference. At five o'clock that morning, they had raided the New Dawn collective—supposedly the aboveground support group of the Berkeley underground Emiliano Zapata Unit—and accompanying a press release about the evidence seized were photographs still wet with developing fluid. Charles Bates held the photos up in the air.

"Mr. Bates," a photographer requested, "real close to your head, please."

Bates proceeded to pose with the photos like Henry Fonda doing a camera commercial. Was there a search warrant? No, but they had a "consent to search" signed by the owner of the house, Judy Sevenson, who later admitted to being a paid FBI informant.

Not only did the raid seem timed to break into print simultaneously with the Sunday funnies, but the investigative technique also smacked of comic-strip morality. In *Dick Tracy*, the "Crimestoppers Textbook" depicted a trio of stereotypical hippie terrorists preparing a time bomb, underscored by the question, "Would you deny police access to knowledge of persons planning your demise?"

Almost six weeks after that Saturday-morning raid, I received a letter by registered mail on Department of Justice stationery:

> Dear Mr. Krassner:
>
> Subsequent to the search of a residence in connection with the arrest of six members of the Emiliano Zapata Unit, the Federal Bureau of Investigation, San Francisco, has been attempting to contact you to advise you of the following information:
>
> During the above-indicated arrest of six individuals of the Emiliano Zapata Unit, an untitled list of names and addresses of

individuals was seized. A corroborative source described the above list as an Emiliano Zapata Unit "hit list," but stated that no action will be taken, since all of those who could carry it out are in custody.

Further, if any of the apprehended individuals should make bail, they would only act upon the "hit list" at the instructions of their leader, who is not and will not be in a position to give such instructions.

The above information is furnished for your personal use and it is requested it be kept confidential. At your discretion, you may desire to contact the local police department responsible for the area of your residence.

Very truly yours,
Charles W. Bates
Special Agent in Charge

But I was more logically a target of the government than of the Emiliano Zapata Unit—unless, of course, they happened to be the same. Was the right wing of the FBI warning me about the left wing of the FBI? Did the handwriting on the wall read *COINTELPRO Lives*? (COINTELPRO was their Counter-Intelligence Program.) Questions about the authenticity of the Zapata Unit had been raised by its first public statement in August 1975, which included the unprecedented threat of violence against the Left.

When a Safeway supermarket in Oakland was bombed by the Zapata Unit, they claimed to have called radio station KPFA and instructed them to notify police, so they could evacuate the area, but KPFA staffers insisted they never received such a call. Now *The Urban Guerrilla*, aboveground organ of the underground NWLF, commented:

> Without offering any proof, the FBI has claimed that [those arrested] were members of the Emiliano Zapata Unit and mistakenly claimed that the Zapata Unit was part of the New World Liberation Front. These FBI claims and lies have been widely repeated by the media.
>
> As soon as they were arrested, Greg Adornetto, whom we knew as Chepito, was separated from the others and disappeared . . .
>
> A close analysis of all the actions and statements . . . by Chepito leads [us] to the inescapable conclusion that he is not just a weak informer, he is a government infiltrator/provocateur. No other conclusion is possible when one considers that he led our comrades to a house he *knew* was under surveillance . . . carrying along things like explosives and half-completed communiqués . . .
>
> He recruited sincere and committed revolutionaries who wanted to participate in being a medium for dialogue with the underground, got a bunch of them in the same room with guns, communiqués and explosives, or even got some of them involved in

> armed actions, and then had . . . Bates move in
> with his SWAT team and bust everybody . . .

In addition, a communiqué from the central command of the NWLF charged that "the pigs led and organized" the Zapata Unit. "We were reasonably sure that it was a set–up from the beginning and we *never* sent one communiqué to New Dawn because of our suspicions."

After publishing the FBI's warning letter to me in the *Berkeley Barb*, I received letters from a couple of members of the Emiliano Zapata Unit in prison. One stated:

> I was involved in the aboveground support
> group of the Zapata Unit. Greg Adornetto led
> myself and several others to believe we were
> joining a cell of the Weather Underground,
> which had a new surge of life when it pub-
> lished *Prairie Fire*. I knew nothing about a hit
> list or your being on one, and can't imagine
> why you would have been. When we were
> arrested, FBI agent-provocateur Adornetto
> immediately turned against the rest of us and
> provided evidence to the government.

Another Zapata Unit prisoner advised:

> You shouldn't have believed the boys in the
> black shiny shoes (FBI) about being on a
> Zapata hit list. They just found some address-
> es, and Bates and his running partner Hearst
> wanted to build up some sensationalism to

take the heat off of Patty's trial. They had over
75 people (politicians and corporate execs)
under protection, thinking all of us didn't get
arrested.

Jacques Rogiers—the aboveground courier for the
underground New World Liberation Front who delivered
their communiqués—told me that the reason I was on the
hit list was because I had written that Donald DeFreeze
was a police informer.

"But that was true," I said. "It's a matter of record.
Doesn't that make any difference?"

It didn't.

"If the NWLF asked me to kill you," Rogiers admitted, "I would."

"Jacques," I replied, "I think this puts a slight damper
on our relationship."

• • •

While the jury was deliberating, I had taken my twelve-
year-old daughter Holly to the empty courtroom, and she
sat in Patty Hearst's chair. But when Mae Brussell phoned
me, worrying that *our* daughters might be kidnapped, I
passed her message on to Holly and offered to accompany
her to school.

"Oh, Daddy," she said, "that's not necessary. Mae's just
paranoid."

Holly then bought a gift for me—a plastic clothespin-
like paper-holder labeled *Threats*. But now, in the face of
Jacques Rogiers's warning, I had to find another place to

live and not tell him my new address, where I kept the FBI's hit-list letter in that *Threats* holder.

On one hand, there was Mae Brussell, dedicated to documenting the rise of fascism in America. On the other hand, there was Holly, standing on her best friend Pia Hinckle's front porch, yelling, "Hitler! Hitler!" That was the name of Pia's cat, so named because of a square black patch under its nose, just like the mustache on Adolf Hitler's face.

I asked Holly, "Do you know who Hitler *was*?"

"Didn't he lead the Jews out of Germany?"

"Well, not exactly . . ."

In the summer of 1977, I got a magazine assignment to cover the trial of Roman Polanski. Holly was now thirteen—the same age as the girl Polanski was accused of seducing (I didn't know yet that it was actually rape)—and she had decided to come to Santa Monica with me, sit in the front row of the courtroom, and just stare at Polanski. She also planned to write an article about the trial from *her* point of view. However, Polanski pleaded guilty to a lesser charge, *then* fled the country on the day he was supposed to be sentenced.

I told Holly, "I'm gonna write about the trial anyway."

"How can you do that?"

"I'll just make it up as if it actually occurred. Roman Polanski's defense will be that the statutory rape laws are unconstitutional because they discriminate against kids."

"How would you feel if the kid was *me*?"

"Well, I'm a liberal father, but . . . you're right. I'm not gonna write the article."

•••

After Patty Hearst was arrested, she had a conversation with a visitor, her best friend since childhood, Trish Tobin, whose family, incidentally, controlled the Hibernia Bank that Patty had supposedly helped rob. Several times throughout the trial, prosecutor Browning attempted to have the tape of that jailhouse dialogue played for the jury, but Judge Carter kept refusing—until the end of the trial, when the impact of its giddiness would be especially astonishing.

> **Trish:** "I had a lot of fights at Stanford."
> **Patty:** "Oh, yeah? About what?"
> **Trish:** "You."
> **Patty:** "Oh—what were they saying? I can just imagine."
> **Trish:** "Oh, well, 'that fucking little rich bitch'—you know, on and on—and they said, 'She planned her own kidnapping,' and I said, 'Fuck you, you don't know what the fuck you're talking about. I don't even care if she plans her kidnapping and everyone's in the world, so you know something, I don't wanna hear shit out of you!" [*Laughter*]

The gossip was that Patty had arranged her own kidnapping in order to get out of her engagement to Steven Weed in as adventurous a way as possible. "I guess I was having second thoughts," she admitted. "I wasn't sure he was somebody I could stay married to"—but that she was then double-crossed and manipulated into becoming an informer.

In any event, Patty's jailhouse tape appeared to reveal a change in her outlook: "I'm not making any statements until I know that I can get out on bail, and then if I find out that I can't for sure, then I'll issue a statement, but I'd just as soon give it myself, in person, and then it'll be a revolutionary feminist perspective totally. I mean I never got really . . . I guess I'll just tell you, like, my politics are real different from, uh—way back when [*laughter*]—obviously! And so this creates all kinds of problems for me in terms of a defense."

An accurate forecast. So at her trial Patty testified that she was influenced to say all that because captured SLA member Emily Harris was in the visiting room at the time Patty was talking to Trish Tobin.

Bailey asked, "Was she a party to your conversation?"

"Not by any intention of ours, no."

On cross-examination, Patty continued: "Emily was also on a phone." Prisoners and visitors had to converse over telephones while they looked at each other through a thick bulletproof-glass window. Patty said she knew that Emily could hear her talking simply because "I could've heard her if I'd stopped and listened." But jail records showed that Emily was *not* in the visiting room then.

While psychiatrist Harry Kozol was testifying in court, Patty was writing notes to Albert Johnson on a yellow legal pad. Later, while I diverted the head marshal's attention by acting suspiciously during recess, reporter Steve Rubinstein copied those notes, but he wasn't allowed to include them in his story for the *Los Angeles Herald Examiner*, a Hearst paper.

In one of the notes, Patty described life in Berkeley with Weed: "I paid the rent, bought the furniture, bought the groceries, cooked all the meals (even while working eight hours a day and carrying a full course load), and if I wasn't there to cook, Steve didn't eat."

In another note, she clearly and concisely described where her mindset really was at in the San Mateo County Jail when she couldn't blame Emily Harris's eavesdropping as her motivation:

"Dr. Kozol kept trying to equate the women's movement with violence. I repeatedly told him: 1. Violence has no place in the women's movement. 2. I didn't feel it was possible to make lasting changes in our society unless the issue of women's rights was resolved. Kozol kept trying to say things like, 'Isn't it more important to solve the poverty problem?' Any reform measures taken by the government will only be temporary."

●●●

Although news items about the trial were clipped out of the daily papers by U.S. marshals, the sequestered jurors were not immune to media influence. During the trial, they all went out to see a few films, selections which they voted on.

They saw *One Flew Over the Cuckoo's Nest*, which, Ken Kesey complained, made Big Nurse the target and omitted the central theme of his book, that people go crazy in this country precisely because they can't handle the gap between the American Dream and the American Nightmare as orchestrated by the same combination that Patty was forced to experience, where organized crime and organized crime-fighting are merely different sides of the same corporate coin.

The jury also saw *Swept Away . . .* reinforcing the theme that one does not transcend one's class unless one is already heading in that direction before circumstances temporarily shatter all those arbitrary rules that distinguish the classes.

And the jury saw *Taxi Driver*—once again perpetuating the myth of the lone nut assassin, played by Robert DeNiro, who, in this case, attempts to kill a political candidate, not because he has been hired by an intelligence agency, but rather because Cybil Shepherd won't stay and hold his hand at a porn movie.

Bill and Emily Harris let it be known that, if called to testify, they would take the Fifth Amendment, but Emily testified, in effect, through the media. After Patty told the jury that Willie Wolfe had raped her, Emily was quoted in *New Times*: "Once, Willie gave her a stone relic in the shape of a monkey face [and] Patty wore it all the time around her neck. After the shootout, she stopped wearing it and carried it in her purse instead, but she always had it with her."

Prosecutor James Browning read that in the magazine, and he had an *Aha!* experience, remembering that "rock" in Patty's purse from the inventory list when she was originally captured. He presented it as his final piece of evidence in the trial, slowly swinging the necklace back and forth in front of the jurors, as if to hypnotize them.

• • •

Patty Hearst had once told a nun to go to Hell, but during the trial her monkey-face necklace was replaced by a religious symbol. It didn't help. The jury found her guilty of being a bank robber—that is, a *virtual* bank robber.

They also found her guilty of fucking when she was fifteen years old—or why else would such information have been admissible as evidence during the trial? They don't allow that kind of testimony in a rape trial, but for a bank robbery it was considered relevant.

Judge Carter sentenced her to thirty-five years, pending the results of ninety days of psychiatric testing. He announced, "I intend to reduce the sentence. How much, I am not now prepared to say."

If you were Patty, would you have answered True or False to the following statements:

> * "My way of doing things is apt to be misunderstood by others."

> * "I am always disgusted with the law when a criminal is freed through the arguments of a smart lawyer."

> * "I feel that it is certainly best to keep my mouth shut when I'm in trouble."

Those are samples from the MMPI, a psychological test Patty had to take. In order to have her sentence reduced, she was required to undergo a psychiatric debriefing extended to six months. Kidnapped again. While Patty was still being probed by the shrinks, Judge Carter died, and the joke was that his replacement would sentence Patty to working as a teller at the Hibernia Bank for rehabilitative purposes.

Eventually, she faced seven years in prison, but after serving twenty-three months, her sentence was commuted by President Jimmy Carter.

Graffiti remained as mute testaments to the whole misadventure. With the same passion that some had previously spray-painted *Free Squeaky* and *Gravity Is the Fourth Dimension*, others left messages like *Jail Rocky and Nixon Not Tania* and *SLA LIVES*, which was then obscured in the enigmatic made-over *COLE SLAW LIVES* slogan that baffled tourists and convinced one visiting ex-Berkeleyite that a political activist named Cole Slaw was dead because there were graffiti saying he was alive.

Finally, although James Browning had once informed me that the Black Panthers were "an organization which advocates killing people" and that Groucho Marx's "utterance did not constitute a 'true' threat," it had since come out that the FBI itself published pamphlets in the name of the Panthers advocating the killing of cops, and that an FBI file on Groucho was indeed begun, and he actually *was* labeled a "national security risk." I called Groucho to tell him the good news. "I deny everything," he said, "because I lie about everything." He paused, then added, "And everything I *deny* is a lie."

THE CASE OF THE TWINKIE MURDERS

JIM JONES, FOUNDER OF the eight-thousand-member People's Temple in San Francisco, once asked Margo St. James, founder of the prostitutes' rights group, COYOTE (Call Off Your Old Tired Ethics), how he could obtain political power.

She answered, sardonically, "Arrange for some of your women to have sex with the bigwigs."

Jones in turn offered to supply busloads of his congregation for any protest demonstration that COYOTE organized, but Margo declined his offer.

"I never liked him," she told me. "I never saw his eyes. Even in the dimmest light, he never removed his shades. He was hiding something. I figured it was his real feelings. I thought he was a slimy creep."

Margo's instincts were correct.

Potential recruits for People's Temple were checked out in advance by Jones's representatives, who would rummage through their garbage and report to him on their findings—discarded letters, food preferences and other clues.

Temple members would visit their homes, and while one would initiate conversation, the other would use the bathroom, copying names of doctors and types of medicine.

They would also phone relatives of a recruit in the guise of conducting a survey and gather other information that would all be taped to the inside of Jones's podium, from which he would proceed to demonstrate his magical powers at a lecture by "sensing the presence" of an individual, mentioning specific details.

When People's Temple moved to Guyana and became Jonestown, Jim Jones would publicly humiliate his followers. For example, he required them to remove their clothing and participate in boxing matches, pitting an elderly person against a young one. He forced one man to participate in a homosexual act in the presence of his girlfriend. There were paddle beatings and compulsory practice-suicide sessions called "White Nights."

On November 18, 1978, Congressman Leo Ryan, who had been investigating Jonestown, was slain at the Guyana airport, along with three newspeople and several disillusioned members of the cult. Jones then orchestrated the mass suicide-murder of nine hundred men, women and children, mostly black.

> **Jones:** "What's going to happen here in a matter of a few minutes is that one of a few on that plane is gonna—gonna shoot the pilot. I know that. I didn't plan it, but I know it's gonna happen. They're gonna shoot that pilot and down comes the plane into the jungle. And we had better not have any of

our children left when it's over 'cause they'll parachute in here on us. So my opinion is that we should be kind to children and be kind to seniors and take over quietly, because we are not committing suicide. It's a revolutionary act."

Christine Miller: "I feel like that as long as there's life, there's hope. There's hope. That's my feeling."

Jones: "Well, someday everybody dies. Someplace that hope runs out 'cause everybody dies."

Miller: "But, uh, I look at all the babies and I think they deserve to live . . ."

Jones: "But also they deserve much more. They deserve peace."

Unidentified man: "It's over, sister, it's over. We've made that day. We made a beautiful day. And let's make it a beautiful day."

Unidentified woman: [*Sobbing*] "We're all ready to go. If you tell us we have to give our lives now, we're ready . . ."

Jones: "The congressman has been murdered—the congressman's dead. Please get us some medication. It's simple. It's simple, there's no convulsions with it, it's just simple. Just please get it before it's too late. The GDF [Guyanese army] will be here. I tell you, get moving, get moving, get moving. How many are dead? Aw, God almighty, God almighty—it's too late, the congressman's dead.

The congressman's aide's dead. Many of our traitors are dead. They're all layin' out there dead."

Nurse: "You have to move, and the people that are standing there in the aisle, go stay in the radio-room yard. So everybody get behind the table and back this way, okay? There's nothing to worry about. So everybody keep calm, and try to keep your children calm. And the older children are to help lead the little children and reassure them. They aren't crying from pain. It's just a little bitter tasting, but that's—they're not crying out of any pain."

Unidentified woman: "I just wanna say something to everyone that I see that is standing around and, uh, crying. This is nothing to cry about. This is something we could all rejoice about. We could be happy about this."

Jones: "Please, for God's sake, let's get on with it. We've lived—let's just be done with it, let's be done with the agony of it. [*There is noise, confusion and applause.*] Let's get calm, let's get calm. [*There are screams in the background.*] I don't know who fired the shot, I don't know who killed the congressman, but as far as I'm concerned, I killed him. You understand what I'm saying? I killed him. He had no business coming. I told him not to come. Die with respect. Die with a degree of dignity. Don't lay down with tears and agony. Stop this hysterics.

This is not the way for people who are social-istic communists to die. No way for us to die. We must die with some dignity.

"Children, it's just something to put you to rest. Oh, God! [*Crying in the background*] I tell you, I don't care how many screams you hear, I don't care how many anguished cries, death is a million times preferable to ten more days of this life. If you'll quit telling them they're dying, if you adults will stop this nonsense—I call on you to quit exciting your children when all they're doing is going to a quiet rest. All they're doing is taking a drink they take to go to sleep. That's what death is, sleep. Take our life from us. We laid it down. We got tired. We didn't commit suicide. We committed an act of revolutionary suicide, protesting the conditions of an inhuman world . . ."

Those who refused to drink the grape-flavored punch laced with potassium cyanide were either shot or killed by injections in their armpits. Jim Jones either shot himself or was murdered.

The *Black Panther* newspaper editorialized: "It is quite possible that the neutron bomb was used at Jonestown."

• • •

Meanwhile, in San Francisco, former policeman Dan White had resigned from the Board of Supervisors because he couldn't support his wife and baby on a salary of $9,600 a year. He obtained a lease for a fast-food franchise at Fisherman's Wharf and now planned to devote himself full time to his new restaurant, The Hot Potato. He felt great relief.

However, White had been the swing vote on the Board, representing downtown real-estate interests and the conservative Police Officers Association. With a promise of financial backing, White changed his mind and told Mayor George Moscone that he wanted his job back.

At first, Moscone said sure, a man has the right to change his mind.

But there was opposition to White's return, led by Supervisor Harvey Milk, who was openly gay. Milk had cut off his ponytail and put on a suit so that he could work within the system, but he refused to hide his sexual preference. Now he warned the pragmatic Moscone that giving the homophobic White his seat back would be seen as an anti-gay move in the homosexual community. White had cast the only vote against the gay rights ordinance.

Even a mayor who wants to run for re-election has the right to change his mind.

On Sunday evening, November 26, a reporter telephoned Dan White and said, "I can tell you from a very good source in the mayor's office that you definitely are *not* going to be reappointed. Can you comment on that?"

"I don't want to talk about it," White replied. "I don't know anything about that." And he hung up.

He stayed on the couch that night, not wanting to keep his wife awake. He didn't get any sleep, just lay there brooding. He decided to go to City Hall on Monday morning.

When his aide, Denise Apcar, picked him up at at 10:15 a.m., White didn't come out the front door as he normally would; he emerged from his garage. He had gone down there to strap on his service revolver, a .38 special, which he always kept loaded. He opened a box of extra cartridges, which were packed in rows of five, and he put ten of them, wrapped in a handkerchief so they wouldn't rattle, into his pocket.

Because of rumors that People's Temple assassins had been programmed to hit targets back in the States, metal detectors were now set up at the front doors of City Hall. When White went up the stairs to the main entrance, he didn't recognize the security guard monitoring the metal detector, so he went around to the side of the building. He entered through a large basement window and proceeded to the mayor's office.

After a brief conversation, Dan White shot George Moscone twice in the body, then two more times in the head, execution-style, as he lay on the floor. The Marlboro cigarette in Moscone's hand would still be burning when the paramedics arrived.

After murdering Moscone, White hurriedly walked down a long corridor to the area where the supervisors' offices were. His name had already been removed from the door of his office, but he still had a key. He went inside and reloaded his gun. Then he walked out, past Supervisor Dianne Feinstein's office. She called out to him, but he didn't stop.

"I have to do something first," he told her.

Harvey Milk was in his office, thanking a friend who had just loaned him $3,000. Dan White walked in.

"Can I talk to you for a minute, Harvey?"

White followed Milk into his inner office. White then fired three shots into Harvey Milk's body, and while Milk was prone on the floor, White fired two more shots into Milk's head.

•••

Meanwhile, Abbie Hoffman had gone underground, and I was scheduled to be a guest on Tom Snyder's late-night TV talk show, *Tomorrow*, on November 30.

"That's my birthday," said Abbie, calling from somewhere or other. "Would you wish me a happy birthday on the show?"

Andy Friendly, producer of the *Tomorrow* show, phoned me to explore areas that the interview might cover. The subject of drug use came up.

"Well," I said, "maybe we could talk about my old psychedelic macho. I've taken LSD in all kinds of unusual situations: when I testified at the Chicago Conspiracy Trial; on the Johnny Carson show—Orson Bean was the guest host— I was sort of a guide for Groucho Marx once; and while I was researching the Charles Manson case, I took acid with a few of the women in the family, including Squeaky Fromme and Sandra Good. It was a kind of participatory journalism."

I didn't tell him that I planned to ingest magic mushrooms before my appearance on the *Tomorrow* show.

They flew me down to Los Angeles, and a chauffeured limousine delivered me to a fancy hotel, where I proceeded to partake of those magic mushrooms. My mood was soon intensely sensual. What I really wanted was an exquisite, deep-tissue massage. I called an old friend who was a professional masseuse. Since she was also an old lover, it wasn't totally surprising that we began fucking on the bed before she even set up her table. She finally broke the sweet silence of our post-coital afterglow.

"But," she said, "I'll have to charge you for the massage."

The mushrooms were still coming on strong when Tom Snyder began the interview. He had an FM mind in an AM body.

"You're from San Francisco" he said. "What the hell is going *on* there? First, this guy Jim Jones has nine hundred people commit suicide by drinking poisoned Kool-Aid. Then the next week this other guy goes to City Hall, kills the mayor and a gay supervisor."

It seemed as if he was asking me to *justify* San Francisco as the cause of such sequential horror.

"Nyah, nyah," I chanted, "my city is more violent than your city."

Snyder looked askance at Andy Friendly, as if to say, "What kind of *flake* did you book for me?"

"Actually," I said, "I believe that Jonestown was a CIA mind-control experiment that got out of control."

"Oh, so you're paranoid, huh?"

"Well, conspiracy and paranoia are not synonymous, you know. But I'll tell you a good conspiracy theory. Remember that famous race-horse, Ruffian? She broke her leg in a race, and they had to shoot her. Well, do you know why they *really* shot Ruffian?"

"No, Paul," Snyder said, knitting his impressive eyebrows in mock consternation. "Why?"

"Because she knew too much."

Snyder did a double-take, then started laughing as though he were doing his impression of Dan Aykroyd on *Saturday Night Live* doing *his* impression of Tom Snyder. I could see Snyder's staccato laughter parading before me like musical notes.

Just before the show ended, I remembered to wish Abbie Hoffman a happy birthday.

"Where is he?" Snyder asked. "Can we get him on the show?"

"He's right there, under your chair."

• • •

When San Francisco District Attorney Joe Freitas learned of the City Hall killings, he was in Washington, DC, conferring with the State Department about the mass suicide-murder in Jonestown. He immediately assumed that Moscone and Milk had been assassinated by a People's Temple hit squad. After all, George Moscone was number one on their hit list.

Freitas had been a close friend of Jim Jones. After the massacre in Guyana, he released a previously "confidential" report, which stated that his office had uncovered evidence to support charges of homicide, child abduction, extortion, arson, battery, drug use, diversion of welfare funds, kidnapping, and sexual abuse against members of the sect. The purported investigation had not begun until after Jones left San Francisco. No charges were ever filed, and the People's Temple case was put on "inactive status."

Busloads of illegally registered People's Temple members had voted in the 1975 San Francisco election, as well as in the runoff that put George Moscone in office. Freitas appointed lawyer Tim Stoen to look into possible voter fraud. At the time, Stoen was serving as Jim Jones's chief legal adviser. Freitas later piously accused him of short-circuiting the investigation, but after Stoen left the case, the D.A.'s office assured the registrar that there was no need to retain the voting rosters, and they were destroyed.

Several former members of People's Temple had heard about this fraudulent voting, but the eyewitnesses all died at Jonestown. In addition, the *San Francisco Examiner* reported that Mayor Moscone had called off a police investigation of gun-running by the Temple, which had arranged to ship explosives, weapons and large amounts of cash to South America via Canada.

George Moscone's body was buried. Harvey Milk's body was cremated. His ashes were placed in a box, which was wrapped in *Doonesbury* comic strips, then scattered at sea. The ashes had been mixed with the contents of two packets of grape Kool-Aid, forming a purple patch on the Pacific. Harvey would've liked that touch.

• • •

In 1979, I covered the Dan White trial for the *San Francisco Bay Guardian*. There was a certain sense of being back in elementary school. Reporters received written instructions: "Members of the press are asked to line up in the below order to facilitate courtroom entry. You must be in the below order or you will be sent to the rear of the line."

I'm embarrassed to admit that I said "Thank you" to the sheriff's deputy who frisked me before I could enter the courtroom. These official friskers each had their own individual style of frisking, and there was a separate-but-equal female frisker for female reporters. But this was a superfluous ritual, since any journalist who wanted to shoot White was prevented from doing so by wall-to-wall bulletproof glass. It was sort of like sitting in a giant New York City taxicab.

At the pre-trial hearings, White had worn standard jailhouse fashion, an orange jumpsuit, so that the first time he walked into court wearing a regular suit and tie, his mother was pleasantly surprised and said, "Oh, my goodness." There was almost an air of festivity, but when the jury selection began next day, White's mother could be observed uttering a silent prayer to herself.

Defense attorney Douglas Schmidt objected to the dismissal of potential jurors because they were opposed to the death penalty. He cited studies showing that those "who do not have scruples against capital punishment tend to favor the prosecution."

Prosecutor Tom Norman claimed that he did not "subscribe to the accuracy of those studies." Judge Walter Calcagno ruled in favor of Norman, and Schmidt was reduced to asking such conscientious objectors if they might at least make an exception in a trial where, say, someone "tortured two or three children to death, for money."

Nor did the defense want any pro-gay sentiment polluting the verdict. Schmidt wasn't allowed to ask potential jurors if they were gay, so instead he would ask if they had ever supported controversial causes—"like homosexual rights, for instance."

There was one particular prospective juror who came from a family of police—ordinarily, Schmidt would have craved for such a person to be on this jury—but when the man mentioned, perhaps gratuitously, "I live with a roommate and lover," it allowed for Schmidt to phrase his next question.

"Where does he or she work?"

The answer began, "He"—and the ballgame was already over—"works at Holiday Inn."

Throughout the trial, White would just sit there as though he had been mainlining epoxy glue. His sideburns were shorter than they used to be. He stared directly ahead, his eyes focused on the crack between two adjacent boxes on the clerk's desk, Olde English type identifying them as "Deft" and "Pltff" for defendant and plaintiff.

When White left the courtroom, there seemed to be no real contact with his wife, save for a glance reminiscent of that time she served the wrong brand of coffee. The front row was reserved for his family, being filled on different days by various combinations of his sixteen brothers and sisters. It felt like I was in the middle of a situation comedy that was morphing into a tragic soap opera.

Although it was stipulated that Dan White had killed George Moscone and Harvey Milk, his defense would be, in effect, that they *deserved* it.

• • •

The day before the trial began, the Assistant District Attorney slated to prosecute the case was standing in an elevator at the Hall of Justice. He heard a voice behind him speak his name.

"Tom Norman, you're a motherfucker for prosecuting Dan White."

He turned around and saw a half-dozen police inspectors. He flushed and faced the door again. These cops were his drinking buddies, but now they were all mad at him.

"I didn't know who said it," Norman confided to the courtroom artist for a local TV station, "and I didn't want to know."

One could only speculate about the chilling effect that incident had on him, conceivably engendering his sloppy presentation of the prosecution's case. For example, in his opening statement, Norman told the jury that White had reloaded his gun in the mayor's office, but not according to the transcript of White's tape-recorded confession.

> **Q.** "And do you know how many shots you fired [at Moscone]?"
> **A.** "Uh, no, I don't, I don't, I out of instinct when I—I reloaded the gun, ah—you know, it's just the training I had, you know."
> **Q.** "Where did you reload?"
> **A.** "I reloaded in my office when, when I was—I couldn't out in the hall."

Which made it slightly less instinctive. Norman sought to prove that the murders had been premeditated, yet ignored this evidence of premeditation in White's own confession. If White's reloading of his gun had been, as he said, "out of instinct," then he indeed *would* have reloaded in Moscone's office. And if it were *truly* an instinctive act, then he would have reloaded *again* after killing Milk.

One psychiatrist testified that White must have been mistaken in his recollection of where he reloaded. The evidence on this key question became so muddled that one juror would later recall, "It was a very important issue, but it was never determined where he reloaded—in Moscone's office or just prior to saying, 'Harvey, I want to talk with you.'"

In his confession, White had stated, "I don't know why I put [my gun] on." At the trial, psychiatrists offered reasons ranging from psychological (it was "a security blanket") to practical (for "self-defense" against a People's Temple hit squad)—this was one week after the Jonestown massacre. But, as a former police officer and member of the Police Commission told me, "An off-duty cop carrying his gun for protection isn't gonna take extra bullets. If he can't save his life with the bullets already in his gun, then he's done for."

Dan White's tearful confession was made to his old friend and former softball coach, Police Inspector Frank Falzon. When Falzon called White "Sir," it was a painful indication of his struggle to be a professional homicide inspector. Now, while Falzon was on the witness stand, one reporter passed a note to her colleague, suggesting that Falzon was wearing a "Free Dan White" T-shirt under his shirt.

At one point in his confession White claimed, "I was leaving the house to talk, to see the mayor, and I went downstairs to—to make a phone call, and I had my gun there." But there was a phone upstairs, and White was home alone. His wife had already gone to the Hot Potato.

But Falzon didn't question him about that. Moreover, he neglected to pose the simple question that any school-kid playing detective would ask: "Dan, who did you call?"—the answer to which could have been easily verified.

Prosecutor Norman simply bungled his case and allowed the defense to use White's confession to its own advantage. The mere transcript could never capture the sound of White's anguish. He was like a little boy sobbing uncontrollably because he wouldn't be allowed to play on the Little League team. When the tape was played in court, some reporters wept, including me, along with members of White's family, spectators, jurors, an assistant D.A.—who had a man-sized tissue box on his table—and Dan White himself, crying both live and on tape simultaneously.

If the prosecution hadn't entered this tape as evidence, the defense could have done so, saving it as the final piece of evidence for dramatic effect.

Yet the heart-wrenching confession was contradicted by White's former aide, Denise Apcar. In his confession, White said that after shooting Moscone, "I was going to go down the stairs, and then I saw Harvey Milk's aide across the hall . . . and then it struck me about what Harvey had tried to do [oppose White's reappointment], and I said, 'Well, I'll go talk to him.'" But Apcar testified that while she was driving White to City Hall, he said he wanted to talk to *both* Moscone and Milk.

On the morning of the murders, although Apcar had let him out of her car at the front entrance to City Hall, he went around the corner to the McAllister Street side and climbed through that basement window because he was carrying a concealed weapon. Now, in court, defense attorney Schmidt was cross-examining a witness as to how many other occasions he had observed such entries being made through this window.

> **A.** "Maybe twenty-five times."
> **Q.** "Then this was not unusual?"
> **A.** "It was usually the same person."

On redirect examination, prosecutor Norman elicited from this witness an admission that he didn't know the name of the individual who entered City Hall through that window, but "always assumed he was an employee, carrying small boxes."

Reporters wondered about the contents of those small boxes. Speculation ranged from cocaine to the parts of a nuclear bomb.

• • •

My daughter Holly and I had moved into a great apartment on States Street, halfway up a long, steep hill, and in the back was what she called "our magic garden."

Our block was just off the intersection of Castro and Market—the heart of the "gay ghetto"—and there was a Chinese laundry at the foot of the hill called the Gay Launderette, which, even though it had changed owners several times, always kept that name for good will.

There was a clothing store named "Does Your Mother Know?" and a bulletin board announcing an "Anal Awareness and Relaxation Workshop," and jokes that gays told about themselves, like, "Why do the Castro clones all have mustaches?" The answer was, "To hide the stretch marks."

I met Harvey Milk when he ran a neighborhood camera shop, and I watched him developing into the gay equivalent of Martin Luther King. Had he lived, he might have been elected the first gay mayor. But he already envisioned the possibility that he would become a martyr. After he was elected supervisor, he taped a message for his constituents, including this prophetic fear and hope: "If bullets should enter my brain, let those bullets blow open every closet door in this country."

The *Los Angeles Times* published a piece by freelancer Mike Weiss which suggested that Dan White's political constituency consisted largely of working-class folks "who are being slowly squeezed out by the advance of a movement whose vanguard is homosexual."

San Francisco Chronicle columnist Charles McCabe quoted from that article in a discussion of what he called "the homosexual invasion" of San Francisco. He went on to make derogatory remarks about White's supposed dealings with blacks on his high school baseball team. He later backed down from these remarks, telling his readers, "I have since concluded these statements cannot be confirmed and I retract them."

White's lawyer had told the *Chronicle* that McCabe's comments were "actionable." Even though White killed the mayor and a supervisor, the *Chronicle* was evidently worried that he might sue the paper for damaging his reputation.

In his election campaign, White had distributed leaflets referring to the problem of "social deviants." But his wife, Mary Ann, explained that "Dan is not against homosexuals—he is one of the most tolerant men. When he said 'social deviants' he didn't mean homosexuals, he meant people who deviate from the social norm, criminals, people who hit somebody over the head, people who jail won't help."

But in court, prosecutor Norman asked Supervisor Carol Ruth Silver if she had ever heard White make any anti-gay statements. She told of his "long diatribe" during a debate about the annual Halloween closing-off of Polk Street—a hostile speech about "how gays' lifestyle had to be contained."

Apparently, White's attorney Schmidt had never said "bullshit" in front of his mother before, but now she was sitting in the courtroom, and on cross-examination he had to use that word in asking Silver if that was how she had characterized the defense in this trial. She had, indeed. Thus was she able to provide the jury with presumably their only input from the outside world. But Schmidt also asked Silver if she herself was "part of the gay community."

She responded, "Are you asking if I'm gay?"

He said, "Yes."

She said, "No."

In the corridor, Schmidt admitted to me that it had been "a ridiculous question."

• • •

Each day of the trial, I would take an hour-long walk from my home to the Hall of Justice. One morning on the news, there was an obituary for the composer of "Happy Days

Are Here Again." I found myself singing it ritualistically on my daily walk to court, even as I passed gas-line after gas-line, every filling station a potential locale for the violence that had already been taking place, every automobile festering with the kind of frustration that could possibly turn a mild-mannered driver into an instant Dan White. He had come to represent the vanguard of vigilante justice in Stress Wars.

A couple of blocks away from the courthouse there was a "Free Dan White" graffito, only it had been altered to read "Freeze Dan White." That may not have been such a bad idea, for he was a missing link in the evolution of our species. He was the personification of obsolescent machismo.

This trial was White's first encounter group, but he never testified in his own defense. Rather, he told his story to several psychiatrists hired by the defense, and *they* repeated those details in court. At a press conference, though, Berkeley psychiatrist Lee Coleman denounced the practice of psychiatric testimony, labeling it as "a disguised form of hearsay."

Mary Ann White sat behind her husband in the front row of spectators, her Madonna-like image in direct view of the jury. Since she was scheduled to testify, prosecutor Norman could have had her excluded from the courtroom. In fact, he could have excluded from the jury George Mintzer, an executive at the Bechtel Company, which had contributed to White's campaign for supervisor. Mintzer became foreman of the jury.

For Mary Ann, this trial was like a Quaker funeral where mourners share anecdotes about the deceased and you find out things you never knew about someone you'd been living with for years. The day after her own tearful testimony, she was back in the front row, taking notes on the testimony of a psychiatrist who had previously interviewed *her* and taken notes. So now she was writing down poignant squibs of *her own recycled observations*, such as "Lack of sex drive" and "Danny didn't intend to shoot anyone."

I had wanted to record testimony, but tape equipment wasn't allowed in the courtroom, although the judge did give permission to vice squad officers to place a recording device on two young boys attending the trial. In court that morning, a sixty-three-year-old man had tried to pick them up.

According to the police report, he had in his possession two vials with "peach colored pills" plus eight white pills. "The juveniles gave details of how the suspect had began [*sic*] a conversation and by passing notes in the courtroom, offered them drugs." Now, three narcotics officers monitored their conversations and later arrested the dirty old man in the Hall of Justice cafeteria.

There was a moment in the trial when it suddenly seemed to be the courtroom incarnation of a TV program called *Make Me Laugh*. Dan White was the contestant, and all the witnesses were attempting to make him laugh. Laurie Parker, a supervisor's aide, almost succeeded. White's demeanor changed perceptibly when she testified that he used to hold the door open for her. Later, she confirmed that "He was smirking at me."

Why was Dan White smirking? Could it have been his awareness of the absurdity that he had slain Moscone and

Milk, yet here was a witness testifying as to his *chivalry*? "Smirking"—the exact same verb that White had used to describe his perception of what Milk did to trigger his own death—just as Jack Ruby had referred to Lee Harvey Oswald's "smirky Communist expression" immediately before he shot Oswald.

• • •

J.I. Rodale, health-food advocate and publishing magnate, once claimed in an editorial in his magazine, *Prevention*, that Lee Harvey Oswald had been seen holding a Coca-Cola bottle only minutes after the assassination of President Kennedy. Rodale concluded that Oswald was not responsible for the killing because his brain was confused. He was a "sugar drunkard." Rodale, who died of a heart attack during a taping of *The Dick Cavett Show*—in the midst of explaining how good nutrition guarantees a long life—called for a full-scale investigation of crimes caused by sugar consumption.

In a surprise move, Dan White's defense team presented just such a bio-chemical explanation of *his* behavior, blaming it on compulsive gobbling down of sugar-filled junk-food snacks. This was a purely accidental tactic. Dale Metcalf, an attorney, told me how he happened to be playing chess with Steven Scherr, an associate of Dan White's attorney.

Metcalf had just read *Orthomolecular Nutrition* by Abram Hoffer. He questioned Scherr about White's diet and learned that, while under stress, White would consume candy bars and soft drinks. Metcalf recommended the book to Scherr, suggesting the author as an expert witness. In his book, Hoffer revealed a personal vendetta against doughnuts, and White had once eaten five doughnuts in a row.

During the trial, psychiatrist Martin Blinder stated that, on the night before the murders, while White was "getting depressed about the fact he would not be reappointed, he just sat there in front of the TV set, bingeing on Twinkies." In my notebook, I scribbled "Twinkie defense," and wrote about it in my next report.

In court, White just sat there in a state of complete control bordering on catatonia, as he listened to an assembly line of psychiatrists tell the jury how *out* of control he had been. One even testified that, "If not for the aggravating fact of junk food, the homicides might not have taken place." And so it came to pass that a pair of political assassinations was transmuted into voluntary manslaughter.

• • •

The Twinkie was invented in 1930 by James Dewar, who described it as "the best darn-tootin' idea I ever had." He got the idea of injecting little cakes with sugary cream-like filling and came up with the name while on a business trip, where he saw a billboard for Twinkle Toe Shoes.

"I shortened it to make it a little zippier for the kids," he said.

In the wake of the Twinkie defense, a representative of the ITT-owned Continental Baking Company asserted that the notion that overdosing on the cream-filled goodies could lead to murderous behavior was "poppycock" and "crap"—apparently two of the artificial ingredients in Twinkies, along with sodium pyrophosphate and yellow dye—while another spokesperson for ITT couldn't believe "that a rational jury paid serious attention to that issue."

Nevertheless, some jurors did. One remarked after the trial that "It sounded like Dan White had hypoglycemia." Doug Schmidt's closing argument became almost an apologetic parody of his own defense. He told the jury that White did not have to be "slobbering at the mouth" to be subject to diminished capacity. Nor, he said, was this simply a case of "eat a Twinkie and go crazy."

Prosecutor Tom Norman's closing argument mixed purple prose—"The defendant had that quality of thought which would embrace the weighing of considerations"—with supercilious sarcasm—"If your friends won't testify for you, who will?"

During the trial, reporter Francis Moriarty had suggested to District Attorney Joe Freitas that prosecutor Norman was blowing the case—echoing similar sentiments by several journalists and attorneys who were monitoring the trial. Freitas passed along the critique to Norman and homicide inspector Frank Falzon.

Falzon challenged Moriarty: "Are you referring to investigative or prosecutorial?"

But the dividing line had become blurred. Falzon sat silently next to Norman at the prosecution table when an ex-cop was allowed on the jury. And neither Falzon nor Norman thought it advisable to subpoena as witnesses those cops with whom Dan White had discussed football shortly after the murders took place and he turned himself in.

When Superior Court Judge Walter Calcagno present-ed the jury with his instructions, he assured them access to the evidence, except that they would not be allowed to have possession of White's gun *and* his ammunition at the same time. After all, these deliberations can get pretty heated. The judge was acting like a concerned schoolteach-er offering Twinkies to students but withholding the cream filling to avoid any possible mess.

On the fiftieth anniversary of the Twinkie, inventor Dewar said, "Some people say Twinkies are the quintes-sential junk food, but I believe in the things. I fed them to my four kids, and they feed them to my fifteen grandchil-dren. Twinkies never hurt them."

Nonetheless, spray-painted on the walls of San Francisco, graffiti cautioned, "Eat a Twinkie—Kill a Cop!"

• • •

After the jury filed out to decide Dan White's fate, specta-tors and reporters alike tried to determine for themselves what could possibly be a fair punishment. The prosecutor kept emphasizing that George Moscone and Harvey Milk were "duly elected"—the wording in Proposition 7 which would enable him to push for the death penalty. Ironically, this case indicated that the death penalty did *not* serve as a deterrent, even for Dan White, who as a supervisor had fought *for* the death penalty because it would serve as a deterrent.

Originally, each juror had to swear eternal devotion to the American criminal justice system. It was that very sys-tem which had allowed for a flimsy, bungled prosecution coupled with a shrewd defense attorney's transmutation of a twin political assassination into the mere White Sugar Murders.

While the jury was out deliberating, reporters passed the time by playing poker or chess, reading books, checking out the porn files in the press room, embroidering sentimental samplers and, mainly, trying to second-guess the jury.

On May 21, 1979, Francis Moriarty brought in a used Ouija board he had purchased at a flea market. The question we reporters asked it was: "When will the verdict come in?" The answer was between 5 and 6.

At 5:25, the jurors walked into court to deliver the verdict. They appeared somber, except for the former cop, who smiled and triumphantly tapped the defense table twice with two fingers as he passed by, telegraphing the decision of voluntary manslaughter. White would be sentenced to only seven years in prison.

"No more Nazi dyke look," the victorious defense attorney announced in the hallway, looking forward to a haircut.

"It was a good fight," the embittered prosecutor pretended, "but we lost."

He should've been grateful the jury had not declared that George Moscone and Harvey Milk were killed in self-defense, or that they had actually committed suicide.

• • •

That evening, I was relaxing at home, smoking a joint, preparing to work on my final report. I remembered how, in 1975, as a state senator, George Moscone had been the author of a bill to decriminalize marijuana.

I was unwinding from the trial and contemplating the implications of the verdict. Patty Hearst had been kidnapped, kept hostage, and brainwashed, yet she was held responsible and was tried for a bank robbery—in which she was forced to participate—and she was sentenced to thirty-five years. Whereas, Dan White had *not* been kidnapped, kept hostage, and brainwashed, yet he was not really held responsible and was tried for assassinating two government officials—voluntarily, after blatant premeditation—and he was sentenced to seven years.

My reverie was suddenly interrupted by a phone call from Mike Weiss. We had become friends during the trial, which he covered for *Time* magazine. He was calling from a phone booth across the street from City Hall. I could hear crowds screaming and sirens wailing behind his voice.

He had to yell: "There's a riot going on! You should get here right away!"

Reluctantly, I took a cab. When I arrived, there were a dozen police cars that had been set on fire, which in turn set off their alarms, underscoring the shouts from a mob of five thousand gays. On the night that Harvey Milk was murdered, they had been among the thirty thousand who marched silently to City Hall for a candlelight vigil. Now they were in the middle of a post-verdict riot, utterly furious.

But where were the cops? They were all fuming *inside* City Hall—where their commander had instructed them to stay—armed prisoners watching helplessly as angry gays broke the glass trying to ram their way through the locked doors.

I spotted Mike Weiss and a student from his magazine-writing class, Marilee Strong. The three of us circulated through the crowd. Standing in the middle of the intersection, *Chronicle* columnist Warren Hinckle was talking with a police official, and he beckoned me to join them. I gathered from their conversation that the cops were about to be released from City Hall. Some were already out. One kept banging his baton on the phone booth where Mike was now calling in his story, and Mike had to wave his press card before the cop would leave.

I found Marilee and suggested that we get away from the area. As we walked north on Polk Street, the police were beginning to march slowly in formation not too far behind us. But the instant they were out of view from City Hall, they broke ranks and started running toward us, hitting the metal pole of a bus stop with their billy clubs, making loud, scary *clangs*.

"We better run," I told Marilee.

"Why? They're not gonna hit us."

"Yes, they are! Run! Hurry!"

The police had been let out of their cage and they were absolutely enraged. Marilee got away, but I was struck with a nightstick on the outside of my right knee. I fell to the ground. The cop ran off to injure as many other cockroaches in his kitchen as he could.

Another cop came charging and he yelled at me, "Get up! Get up!"

"I'm trying to!"

He made a threatening gesture with his billy club, and when I tried to protect my head with my arms, he jabbed me viciously on the exposed right side of my ribs.

Oh, God, the pain!

The cops were running amok now, in an orgy of indiscriminate sadism, swinging their clubs wildly and screaming, "Get the fuck outa here, you fuckin' faggots, you motherfuckin' cocksuckers!"

I managed to drag myself along the sidewalk. It felt like an electric cattle prod was stuck between my ribs. Marilee drove me to a hospital emergency ward.

At the hospital, X-rays indicated that I had a fractured rib and pneumothorax—a punctured lung. There were several others already there who had been beaten in police sweeps. Another wave of victims would soon arrive after the cops carried out a search-and-destroy mission on the customers in a gay bar, Elephant Walk, at Castro and Eighteenth Street.

Although Dan White had acted on his own, he might just as well have been a Manchurian candidate for these cops. When the verdict was first announced, somebody sang "Oh, Danny Boy" over the police radio.

After six weeks of celibacy while the healing process took place, I thought I was ready for sex again, but when my partner embraced me tightly during her climax, I felt a sharp pain and groaned. She got turned on by what she interpreted as a moan of pleasure, and she squeezed me even tighter, which only made me groan louder, turning her on even more. Tighter, louder, tighter, louder. We were riding on a vicious cycle.

The City of San Francisco was sued for $4.3 million by a man who had been a peaceful observer at the riot following the verdict. He was walking away from the Civic Center area when a cop yelled, "We're gonna kill all you faggots!"—and beat him on the head with **a** nightstick. He was awarded $125,000. I had wanted to sue the police myself, but an attorney requested $75 for a filing fee, and I didn't have it. I was too proud to borrow it, and I decided to forego the lawsuit. This was one of the dumbest mistakes of my entire life.

The injuries affected my posture and my gait, and I gradually began to develop more and more of a strange limp.

• • •

In 1982, psychiatrist Martin Blinder—who had helped establish Dan White's Twinkie defense—aided Arizona police officer John Clarke in plea-bargaining his way out of sexual assault, kidnapping, and armed burglary charges. Dr. Blinder testified that the cop had assaulted, bound, and sexually abused a woman while he was suffering from "Fugue State," a disorder which sometimes accompanies hypoglycemia, wild fluctuations in blood sugar.

The psychiatrist testified that the policeman blacked out for ninety minutes while driving his car during a hypoglycemic attack. The officer ate doughnuts daily, up until the day he followed a young woman home from a supermarket, confronted her with his service revolver, forced his way into her residence, tied her up, and fondled her breasts. He said it was only later that night he realized what he had done. He was allowed to plead guilty to second-degree burglary, for which he would receive probation.

In 1983, the *San Francisco Chronicle* published a correction: "In an article about Dan White's prison life,

Chronicle writer Warren Hinckle reported that a friend of White expressed the former supervisor's displeasure with an article in the *San Francisco Bay Guardian* which made reference to the size of White's sexual organ. The *Chronicle* has since learned that the *Bay Guardian* did not publish any such article and we apologize for the error."

It was ten feet long, 3 feet 6 inches high, 3 feet 8 inches wide, and weighed more than a ton—no, not Dan White's penis—the world's largest Twinkie, which was unveiled in Boston.

In January 1984, Dan White was released from prison. He had served a little more than five years for killing Moscone and Milk. The estimated shelf life of a Twinkie is seven years. That's two years longer than White spent behind bars. When he was released, that Twinkie in his cupboard was still edible. But maybe, instead of eating it, he would have it bronzed.

In November 1984, prosecutor Tom Norman was convicted of drunk driving. He had been arrested for driving through a stop sign and over the double line twice. Previously convicted for reckless driving, he now received a one-year suspended sentence.

In June 1985, Sirhan Sirhan told the *Los Angeles Times*: "If [White] had a valid diminished capacity defense because he was eating too many Twinkies, I sure had a better one because of too many Tom Collinses, plus the deep feeling about my homeland that affected my conduct."

In October 1985, Dan White committed suicide by carbon monoxide poisoning in his garage. He taped a note to the windshield of his car, reading: "I'm sorry for all the pain and trouble I've caused." White's defense attorney,

Doug Schmidt, said, "I expected that he would kill himself. And, in certain respects it vindicates the defense. I don't think a well man takes his own life."

• • •

During the trial, an old friend, TV reporter Joyce Shank, who was also covering the trial, came to my house so we could compare notes. While she was visiting, there was an earthquake. She immediately jumped under my desk, just as she had once demonstrated on television what to do in case of an earthquake.

Now she said, "Paul, get under here with me, hurry up."

I quickly hunched next to her under my desk. Our thighs were touching. Was it possible that my secret lust for Joyce might now become fulfilled?

"Put the radio on," she said.

I got up and put the radio on, then joined her again.

"Not *music*," she said, "the *news* . . ."

Okay, now that incident is even more embarrassing than saying "Thank you" to the guy who frisked me in the courthouse, but it served as a catalyst to my understanding of the psychological overtones of the Dan White case, because it's such a blatant example of how the process of projection can affect your perception, your empathy, your rationality, your behavior.

And, indeed, it was the lustfulness of George Moscone and Harvey Milk which may have underlain the more obvious motivation that sexually inadequate Dan White had in destroying them. It was well known around City Hall that Moscone had a predilection for black women. Police almost arrested him once with a black prostitute in a car at a supermarket parking lot. And Milk had once told White, "Don't knock [gay sex] unless you've tried it." When political opponent John Briggs debated Milk, Briggs perpetuated a stereotype of gay promiscuity with a statistic that 25 percent of gay men had over five hundred sexual contacts.

"I wish," said Harvey.

• • •

Over the years, I developed an increasingly unbalanced walk, triggered by that police beating, so that my right foot would come down hard on the ground with each step. My whole body felt twisted, and my right heel was in constant pain.

I limped the gamut of therapists—from an orthodox orthopedic surgeon who gave me a shot of cortisone in my heel to ease the pain, to a specialist in neuromuscular massage who wondered if the cop had gone to medical school because he knew exactly where to hit me with his billy club, to a New Age healer. She put one hand on my stomach, held the receptionist's hand with the other, and asked her whether I should wear a brace. The answer was yes. I decided to get a second opinion—perhaps from another receptionist.

Meanwhile, my twisted limp became increasingly worse. In 1987 I went to a chiropractor, who referred me to a podiatrist, who referred me to a physiatrist, who wanted me to get an MRI—a CAT scan—in order to rule out the possibility of cervical stenosis. But the MRI ruled it *in*. The X-rays indicated that my spinal cord was being squeezed by spurring on the inside of several discs in my neck. The physiatrist told me that I needed surgery.

I panicked. I had always taken my good health for granted. I went into heavy denial, confident that I could completely cure my problem by walking barefoot on the beach every day for three weeks.

"You're a walking time bomb," the podiatrist warned me.

He said that if I were in a rear-end collision, or just out strolling and I tripped, my spinal cord could be severed, and I would be paralyzed from the chin down. I began to be conscious of every move I made. I was living, not one day at a time, not one hour at a time, not one minute at a time—I was living one *second* at a time.

I was one of thirty-seven million Americans who didn't have insurance, nor did I have any savings. Fortunately, I had an extended family and friends all over the country who came to my financial rescue. The operation was scheduled to take place at the Hospital for Joint Diseases in New York.

A walking time bomb! I was still in a state of shock, but since I perceived the world through a filter of absurdity, now I would have to apply that perception to my own situation. The breakthrough for me came when I learned that my neurosurgeon moonlighted as a clown at the circus.

"All right, I surrender," I said to myself. "I surrender."

Paralyzed from the chin down! I fantasized about using a voice-activated word processor to write a novel called *The Head*, in which the protagonist finally dies of suffocation while performing cunnilingus because he can't use his hands to separate the thighs of the woman who is sitting on his face.

I met my doctor the night before the operation. He sat on my bed wearing a trench coat and called me Mr. Krassner. I thought that if he was going to cut me open and file through five discs in my upper spinal column, he could certainly be informal enough to call me Paul. He was busy filling out a chart.

"What do you do for a living, Mr. Krassner?"

"I'm a writer and a comedian."

"How do you spell comedian?"

Rationally I knew that you don't have to be a good speller to be a fine surgeon, but his question made me uneasy. At least his *hands* weren't shaking while he wrote. Then he told me about how simple the operation was and he mentioned almost in passing that there was always the possibility I could end up staying in the hospital for the rest of my life. *Huh?* There was a time when physicians practiced positive thinking to help their patients, but now it was a requirement of malpractice prevention to provide the worst-case scenario in advance.

The next morning, under the influence of Valium and Demerol, I could see that my neurosurgeon had just come from the circus, because he was wearing a clown costume, with a big round red nose over his surgical mask. He couldn't get close to the operating table because his shoes were so large, and when he had to cleanse my wound he asked the nurse to please pass the seltzer bottle . . .

"Wake up, Paul," the anesthesiologist said, "Surgery's over. Wiggle your toes."

My wife Nancy was waiting in the hall—there she stood, my favorite "biological quirk" (as she described her own existence)—and I was never so glad to see her smile.

That evening, at a benefit in Berkeley, Ken Kesey told the audience, "I spoke with Krassner today, and the operation was successful, but he says he's not taking any painkillers because he never does any legal drugs." Then Kesey led the crowd in a chant: "Get well, Paul! Get well, Paul!" And it worked. The following month I was performing again, wearing a neck brace at a theater in Seattle.

But, over the years, I gradually got gimpier and gimpier. My hip was so out of kilter that my right foot turned inward when I walked, and my left foot continuously was tripping on my right foot. More and more often, I found myself falling all over the place. Dozens of times. Finally, after I started inadvertently knocking down other people like dominoes at a book festival in Australia, I realized that I would definitely need to start walking with a cane. Since then, at any airport, I had to put my cane on the conveyor belt, along with my carry-on bag and my shoes. And then the security guy hands me a *different* cane—a wooden one, painted orange—to help me walk through the metal detector without falling.

One time, in a restaurant, I tripped on my own cane and fell flat on my face—bruising myself badly, yet grateful that I hadn't broken any teeth. That's my nature—to perceive a blessing in disguise as soon as I stop bleeding. However, this time I was left with a dark, square-shaped scab between my nose and my lips. It looked like a Hitler mustache, and I became very self-conscious about it.

Now I really *am* a walking time bomb. I cannot afford to fall again. I must be careful when I walk. I have to be fully conscious of every step. Left. Right. Left. Right. Left. Right. Any fall could injure me. It might even be fatal. I have surrendered to a process that is truly an ongoing lesson in mindfulness. I'm learning that when you are mindful in one aspect of your life, you'll strengthen mindfulness in other aspects. I am, after all, a Zen Bastard—a title bestowed upon me when Ken Kesey and I coedited *The Last Supplement to the Whole Earth Catalog*—and I certainly have no desire to trip while hobbling along my particular path.

• • •

On the twenty-fifth anniversary of the double execution, the *San Francisco Chronicle* reported that, "During the trial, no one but well-known satirist Paul Krassner—who may have coined the phrase 'Twinkie defense'—played up that angle. His trial stories appeared in the *San Francisco Bay Guardian*. 'I don't think Twinkies were ever mentioned in testimony,' said chief defense attorney Douglas Schmidt, who recalls 'HoHos and Ding Dongs,' but no Twinkies."

Apparently, Schmidt forgot that one of his own psychiatric witnesses, Martin Blinder, had used the T-word in his testimony.

Blinder now complains, "If I found a cure for cancer, they'd still say I was the guy who invented 'the Twinkie defense.'"

The *Chronicle* also quoted Steven Scherr about the Twinkie defense: "'It drives me crazy,' said co-counsel Scherr, who suspects the simplistic explanation provides cover for those who want to minimize and trivialize what happened. If he ever strangles one of the people who says

'Twinkie defense' to him, Scherr said, it won't be because he's just eaten a Twinkie."

Scherr was sitting in the audience at the University of San Francisco theater where a panel discussion of the case was taking place. I was one of the panelists. When Scherr was introduced from the stage, I couldn't resist saying to him on my microphone, "Care for a Twinkie?"

• • •

Soon after the Dan White trial, I got a phone call from Lee Cole, an ex-Scientologist I had met in Chicago while researching the Charles Manson case. He wanted to visit me, but I said no.

"Suppose I just come over?" he said.

"You don't know where I live."

"I can find out."

"If you find out, and you tell me how you did, you can come over."

I wanted to determine how carefully I had covered my tracks, or see which friend would give out my address. A little while later, Lee Cole called again and told me my address—he said that he had obtained it from the voter registration files—so I told him to come over.

He took me to see Lowell Streiker, author of *The Cults Are Coming!* and a deprogrammer who had counseled one-third of the Jonestown survivors. In the course of our conversation, I mentioned my theory that Jim Jones had served as a pimp at City Hall and maintained power by implied blackmail.

Dr. Streiker told me of his friend—a member of Jones's planning commission—who had told him about the technique that People's Temple had used on the mayor. They sent a young black female member to service him, as a gift, then called the next week about a serious problem— she had lied, said she was eighteen, when in fact she was underage, but don't worry, we have it under control—just the way J. Edgar Hoover used to manipulate top politicians with his juicy FBI files.

So Jim Jones had taken Margo St. James's sardonic advice after all, on how to achieve political power: "Arrange for some of your women to have sex with the bigwigs." And he had taken it all the way to a mass suicide-murder— which occurred simultaneously with a mass demonstration by the women's movement in San Francisco, called "Take Back the Night!"

They completely shut down traffic on Broadway. But there was not a word about that event in any of the media. It was knocked totally out of the news by the massacre in Jonestown.

When Dan White was paroled in 1984, he called his old friend, Frank Falzon—the detective who had originally taken his confession—and they met. A decade later, Falzon, now in the insurance business, told Mike Weiss about that encounter.

"I hit him with the hard questions," Falzon recalled. "I asked him, 'What were those extra bullets for? What *did* happen?'"

"I really lost it that day," White said.

"You can say that again," Falzon said.

"No. I really lost it. I was on a mission. I wanted four of them."

"Four?" Falzon said.

"Carol Ruth Silver—she was the biggest snake of the bunch." Silver realized that she might have been his third victim had she not stayed downstairs for a second cup of coffee that morning. "And Willie Brown. He was master-minding the whole thing."

While White had been waiting to see George Moscone in the anteroom of his office, the mayor was drinking coffee with Willie Brown, chatting and laughing. Finally, Moscone told Brown that he had to see Dan White. Brown slipped out the back door just as Moscone was letting White in the front way. Thirty seconds later, White killed Moscone.

Dianne Feinstein, who was president of the Board of Supervisors, succeeded Moscone as mayor and is now a senator. Willie Brown later became the mayor of San Francisco. Jonestown and Kool-Aid continue to serve as occasional joke references for stand-up comedians and metaphors for politicians and pundits alike.

As for me, my physical condition has gotten worse, including my balance, and I've had to substitute a walker for my cane. I exercise at a gym three times a week, but they won't allow me to use my walker on the treadmill.

REFLECTIONS OF A REALIST

PAUL KRASSNER INTERVIEWED BY TERRY BISSON

Your first gig was with Mad *magazine, right? How did that come about?*

Actually, my first gig was when I was a kid working in a grocery store, separating cherries with green mold from the plain red ones. It was a kind of meditation. In my last year of college, I began working for *The Independent*, an anti-censorship paper, where I eventually became managing editor. The publisher, Lyle Stuart, was friends with Bill Gaines, the publisher of *Mad*, and when Gaines hired Stuart as his business manager, we moved our office downtown to what was unofficially known as "the Mad building."

I wasn't on the staff of *Mad*, but I wrote some scripts on a freelance basis. The premise of my first submission was "What if comic-strip characters answered those little ads in the back of magazines?" But the editor—Al Feldstein, who replaced Harvey Kurtzman—wouldn't include Good Old Charlie Brown responding to the "Do

You Want Power?" ad, because he didn't think the *Peanuts* strip was well-known enough yet to parody. Nor would Popeye's flat-chested girlfriend, Olive Oyl, be permitted to send away for a pair of falsies.

Bill Gaines said, "My mother would object to that."

"Yeah," I said, "but she's not a typical subscriber."

"No, but she's a typical mother."

I sold a few other ideas to *Mad*, but when I suggested a satire on the pros and cons of unions, Feldstein wasn't interested in even seeing it because the subject was "too adult." Since *Mad*'s circulation had already gone over the million mark, Gaines intended to keep aiming the magazine at teenagers.

"I guess you don't wanna change horses in midstream," I said.

"Not when the horse has a rocket up its ass," Gaines replied.

At that time, there was no satirical magazine for grown-ups—like *Punch* in England or *Krokodil* in the Soviet Union or *Oz* in Australia—and so when I launched *The Realist* in 1958, I didn't have any competition. But I also had no role models for such a magazine. I just made it up as I went along.

Was the success of The Realist *a surprise?*

Yeah, absolutely. I thought it might reach a thousand circulation. And when it did, then I hoped it might reach three thousand. In two years, it did. Later, five thousand. Then ten thousand. Then twenty-five. Then fifty thousand. In 1967, the circulation peaked at a hundred thousand. And the pass-on readership was estimated at two million. But who really knows how many?

In any case, the readers had in common a sense of irreverence toward piety and pomposity. My credo was to communicate without compromise. I had no publisher or advertisers to answer to. The subscribers and newsstand buyers trusted me not to be afraid of offending them. And their urge to share fueled that Malthusian growth of *The Realist*. Word-of-mouth was the best kind of advertising and it was free.

Is there anything in your view that replaces The Realist *today?*

Well, because *The Realist* was personal, unique, originally published in the context of a blossoming counterculture, and undermined by the FBI's COINTELPRO (Counter-Intelligence Program), I say with all the false humility I can muster that *nothing* can replace *The Realist*. As for satirical publications, there's been *National Lampoon* and *Spy* magazine. And later, published in cyberspace, *The Onion*, *The Borowitz Report*, and *Ironic Times*. Incidentally, all issues of *The Realist* are now online at The Realist Archive Project. Meanwhile, irreverence has become an industry.

Ever meet Lord Buckley?

Nope. However, when I moved from New York to San Francisco in 1971 to coedit with Ken Kesey *The Last Supplement to the Whole Earth Catalog*, I also hosted my own radio program on ABC's FM station. My first appearance was on the morning of Easter Sunday, so I opened with Lord Buckley's classic jazzed-up performance of *The Nazz* (that's short for Nazarene).

Have you ever taught comedy? Like in college? Has anybody?

The closest I've come to that was in the '60s when I taught a course at the Free University in New York. It was titled "Journalism and Satire: How to Tell the Difference." There are teachers of comedy now. Perhaps the best is Beth Lapides. I call her the mother of alternative comedy.

What do you think of WikiLeaks?

Well, let me put it this way: I trust WikiLeaks more than Wikipedia. I consider whistleblowers like Julian Assange, Chelsea (formerly Bradley) Manning, and Edward Snowden to be heroic figures on an international level. In the '60s, we wore buttons that said *No Secrets* and we carried posters that proclaimed *Information Is Free*.

Now, WikiLeaks has been transmutating those abstract ideas into worldwide public scrutiny of clandestine communications, ranging from embarrassing quotes to the revelation of international criminality. Here's an example: The Yemeni president covered up United States drone strikes against al-Qaeda in Yemen. He told General David Petraeus in a diplomatic cable, "We'll continue saying the bombs are ours, not yours"—sort of like vice-presidential candidate John Edwards's assistant claiming to be the father of a baby when actually it was Edwards himself who had impregnated his mistress.

It looks like pot is gradually getting legalized. Does this please you or dismay you?

It pleases my ass off. I mean, why would it dismay me? It dismays the DEA and the prison guards' union. It even dismays some growers, dealers, and medical marijuana dispensaries. In a truly free society, the distinction of whether marijuana is used for medical or recreational purposes would be as irrelevant an excuse for discrimination as whether the sexual preference of gays and lesbians is innate or a matter of choice.

It dismays the Partnership for a Drug-Free America, which was originally founded and funded by the pharmaceutical industry, the alcohol industry, and the tobacco industry. Cigarettes are legal and kill 1,300 people every day—and that's just in this country—but marijuana is still mostly illegal, yet the worst that can happen is maybe you'll get a severe case of the blind munchies and eat a bunch of legal junk food.

What *does* dismay me, though, is that as long as any government can arbitrarily decide which drugs are legal and which are illegal, then anyone serving time for a nonviolent drug offense is a political prisoner. So, even though Colorado and Washington are the first two states to legalize recreational marijuana, I won't be satisfied until amnesty is declared, freeing all those stoners who are still living behind bars.

Incidentally, there was a questionnaire that was published in *High Times*, and one of the questions was, "Is it possible to smoke too much pot?" And a reader answered, "I don't understand the question."

Seems to me that American humor, at least since the fifties, is primarily Jewish. I mean from Milton Berle to Sid Caesar to Lenny Bruce to, hell, Jon Stewart. Not to mention Paul Krassner. What's the deal with that?

First of all, I don't think of myself as Jewish. My parents were, but I consider all religions to be organized superstition. Ironically, anyone who thinks of Judaism as a race rather than a religion is accepting Nazi tenets. I don't believe that Jews were the chosen people, or that humans were the chosen species. If that darned asteroid hadn't rendered all those dinosaurs extinct, would creationists be driving around only in cars fueled by batteries? But although I'm an atheist, I welcome diversity, as long as no theological dogma is allowed to become a law.

Anyway, sure, there was some truth to the stereotype of Jewish comedians, but that's changed. Steve Allen wasn't Jewish. George Carlin wasn't. Richard Pryor wasn't. Chris Rock isn't. Margaret Cho isn't. Conan O'Brien isn't. Louis C.K. was raised as a Catholic but is now an agnostic. Bill Maher is also an agnostic—his father was Catholic, and Bill was a teenager when he learned that his mother was Jewish. Stephen Colbert is a practicing Catholic, and he teaches Sunday School. As for me, I've had my foreskin sewn back on my penis.

Does that still hurt?

Only when I come.

You once described the Diggers as a cross between Mother Teresa and Tim Leary. Was that supposed to be a compliment?

I guess so. They served as social workers for the Haight-Ashbury community in San Francisco, and they took acid trips.

What do you think of hip-hop?

Besides passion and talent in show biz, I think of the hip-hop community as part of the ever-evolving counterculture. In the past several decades, we've gone from bohemians to Beats, from hippies to Yippies, from punk to hip-hop—it's essentially the same spirit continuing in different forms.

Ever been attacked by wild animals?

Only by cops swinging billy clubs and howling triumphantly.

Ever meet Woody Allen?

I interviewed him for *The Realist* in 1965. We concluded:

> **Q.** Are you concerned about the population explosion?
> **A.** No, I'm not. I mean, I recognize it as a problem which those who like that area can fool around with. I doubt if there's anything I can do about the population explosion, or about the atom bomb, besides vote when the time comes, and I contribute money to those organizations who spend their days in active

pursuit of ends that I'm in agreement with. But that's all. And I'm not going to set fire to myself.

Q. But do you agree with the motivation of the Buddhist monks who set fire to themselves in Vietnam?

A. I don't think so. No, I think that they don't know what they're doing. I think they're nuts. That's *not* the answer. When all is said and done, it's not the answer. When you're home at night and you say to yourself, "Tomorrow morning I'll get up at eight o'clock and set fire to myself," there's something wrong. I wouldn't do it that way.

I can see dying for a principle, but not that way. At the very minimum, if you are going to die for something, you should at least take *one of them* with you. Go back to the Jews in Germany. If you have a loaded gun in your home, and the state comes to get you, you can at least get two or three of *them*.

I'm not opposed to violence as a course of action in many instances. Sometimes passive resistance is fine, but violence in its place is a good and necessary thing. But setting fire to yourself is not the answer. With my luck, I would be un-inflammable.

My Jeopardy *answer: "It seemed like a good idea at the time." You provide the question.*

Why did you stop beating your wife?

Watch any TV?

Less and less. Let's see . . . Bill Maher. *The Simpsons. Sixty Minutes. Louie.* Occasional movies or documentaries. If *Curb Your Enthusiasm* were still on, I'd watch. So, instead of Larry David, I watch *Seinfeld* reruns, despite the annoying laugh-track. I watch Rachel Maddow. I watch the real news and the fake news as they borrow clips from each other.

How come you have never hosted the Oscars?

Their invitation must've gotten lost by the Post Office.

Each in one sentence please: Sarah Silverman, Sarah Palin, Thelonious Monk, Andy Warhol.

Sarah Silverman confessed her bedwetting trauma without the aid of a priest. When Sarah Palin was chosen as John McCain's running mate, and CBS interviewed her at home, a member of the crew told me that he saw the potential vice president remove from a shelf a book about seceding from the United States. I once interviewed Thelonious Monk for *Playboy*, and I was tempted to call him Felonious, but I figured that he'd already heard that too many times.

A few decades after Valerie Solanas shot Andy Warhol in 1968, his cohort, Paul Morrissey, said in an interview by Taylor Mead (who had played himself in Warhol's film, *Taylor Mead's Ass*, described in Wikipedia as a "sixty-minute opus that consisted entirely of Taylor Mead's ass, during which Mead first exhibits a variety of movement, then *appears* to shove a variety of objects up his ass") that "Solanas approached underground newspaper publisher Paul Krassner for money, saying, 'I want to shoot [Olympia Press publisher] Maurice Girodias,' and he gave her $50, enough for a .32 automatic pistol," which, of course, Paul Morrissey shoved up Taylor Mead's ass.

What's your favorite gadget?

You mean like my drone that delivers the *Washington Post* to Jeff Bezos? Or my invention of a combination dildo and anti-insomnia gadget called Dildoze? Actually, I like my answering machine, because I can screen all my calls. And as a result, telemarketers—whether they're humans or robots—automatically hang up. If a gadget doesn't have to have moving parts, then I say yay for my back-scratcher.

Was there anyone in the '60s counterculture you didn't meet? What would you say to them today?

Yeah, there were millions of 'em. At the risk of revealing my self-serving streak, I would recommend to them my own memoir (available at paulkrassner.com), *Confessions of a Raving, Unconfined Nut: Misadventures in the Counterculture*, about which Pulitzer Prize winner Art Spiegelman wrote that "His true wacky, wackily true autobiography is the definitive book on the sixties." Oops, wait, you must mean *famous* countercultural icons. Well,

I would've liked to meet Mario Savio. He gave that passionate speech in 1964, outdoors on the steps of Sproul Hall at the UC–Berkeley campus: "There's a time when the operation of the machine becomes so odious, makes you so sick at heart, that you can't take part! You can't even passively take part! And you've got to put your bodies upon the gears and upon the wheels . . . upon the levers, upon all the apparatus, and you've got to make it stop! And you've got to indicate to the people who run it, to the people who own it, that unless you're free, the machine will be prevented from working at all!"

Today I would say to him, "Thanks for inspiring the Free Speech Movement."

I would've also liked to meet Janis Joplin. Actually, I sort of did, but not really. We were both performing in a benefit at the Fillmore East. While I was onstage in the middle of an anecdote, she was walking toward the exit doors, and she was wearing anklets with these bells that rang all the way up the aisle. Later, hurrying out of the theater, she saw me in the lobby. "Hey, I'm sorry about my cowbells," she said, "but I hadda take a leak."

"Oh, that's okay, but ain't it better to *give* then to take?" She cackled and left the building. Today I would say to her, "Belated thanks for your empathy."

Have you ever been tempted to fake your death so you could read your New York Times *obit?*

That wouldn't be necessary, because NPR already has one in the can, and the radio journalist who did it sent me a CD, so I had the rare privilege of fact-checking my own obituary. And recently an AP correspondent was also assigned to prepare my obit. So now I can sign my books with this inscription: "This book will be worth more on eBay when I'm dead."

Three favorite movies?

Network. Sophie's Choice. The Night Porter. And a fourth: *The Producers.* Hmmm. There's a pattern there. Those last three were about Nazi Germany, and the first one was about creeping fascism in America.

Ever read science fiction?

Theodore Sturgeon: We became friends, and he wrote a column for *The Realist.* And when I was at *Hustler*, I appointed him as our book reviewer.

    Harlan Ellison: We also became friends, and he wrote an introduction to my anthology, *Pot Stories for the Soul: An Updated Edition for a Stoned America.* "Basically, fuck dope," he began. "No offense, dude, but fuck dope."

    Octavia Butler: My wife Nancy and I were seated at the same dinner table with her at a literary event, and discussing fiction, she offered a fine bit of advice on finding things to like about an evil character.

You were once the centerfold in Hustler magazine. Any plans for a repeat?

It's not on *my* to-do list. In 1978, after Larry Flynt had converted to Christianity, he hired me to mesh porn and religion. I suggested a scratch-'n'-sniff centerfold of the Virgin Mary. "That's a great idea," he said. "We'll have a portrait of the Virgin Mary, and when you scratch the spot, it'll smell like tomato juice." Anyway, I was completely naked except for wearing my old cowboy hat in the photo you're referring to. It accompanied an interview in *Hustler's* first born-again issue.

You once took LSD with Groucho Marx. So what?

You had to be there. But okay, I'll give you a snippet of the trip. Groucho told me about one of his favorite contestants on *You Bet Your Life:* "He was an elderly gentleman with white hair, but quite a chipper fellow. I asked him what he did to retain his sunny disposition. 'Well, I'll tell you, Groucho,' he says, 'every morning I get up and I *make a choice* to be happy that day.'" Then he went to urinate. When he came back, he said, "You know, everybody is waiting for *miracles* to happen. But the whole *human body* is a goddamn miracle.

Do you regard yourself as a journalist or a satirist?

Both, though I label myself as an investigative satirist. Currently, I'm working on my long-awaited—by me, anyway—first novel, about a contemporary Lenny Bruce–type performer.

Imbedded in your journalism career are two serious crusades: for abortion rights and against cigarettes. Any progress?

In 1962, when abortions were considered a crime, I never thought they would be legalized in my lifetime. After I had published an interview with Dr. Robert Spencer, without identifying him, I began to get calls from women who were pregnant but didn't want to be, and I became an underground abortion referral service, and in the process, morphing from a satirist to an activist. I was subpoenaed by district attorneys in two cities, but I refused to testify before their grand juries. Then came *Roe vs. Wade*, and I never thought that abortions would become a crime again in my lifetime, but now it seems like a possibility, one state at a time. States' rights aren't just for racists any more.

As for cigarettes, in January 2014, the *Los Angeles Times* published my letter to the editor:

> Re "Smoking's global grip," Opinion, Jan. 21. Thomas J. Bollyky writes the following: "Step by step, the government cracked down on tobacco. Warning labels were added to cigarette packages (1965), cigarette advertising was banned on television and radio (1971), smoking on commercial airline flights was forbidden (1987), and tobacco products were put under Food and Drug Administration oversight (2009). . . . U.S. criminal and civil tobacco lawsuits exposed and punished tobacco companies for decades of obfuscation and malfeasance."
>
> And yet that same government still uses taxpayer funds to subsidize the tobacco industry. American schizophrenia rules!

Hmmm. Did you know I was a tobacco farmer in Kentucky back in the '70s?

I do now.

Ever do Burning Man? I mean, you live in the fucking desert anyway.

Okay, please forgive me, but I've never been to Burning Man. Is that a countercultural sin? Do I have to say a hundred Hail Learys?

What kind of car do you drive? (I ask this of everyone.)

I never learned to drive. When I moved to San Francisco, I bought a used Volkswagen convertible for $500, stick shift of course, even though I didn't know how to drive. The hills in San Francisco scared me, and so friends would drive me from place to place in my own car, while I sat on the passenger side and took care of the glove compartment.

Remember Sing Out *magazine?*

Yes, I do. So what?

Are things getting better or worse? Or is that a fair question?

It's a fair question. I wish I had a fair answer, but one person's perception of "better" is another person's perception of "worse." I waver between hope and despair, between the Occupy Wall Street progressives and the Tea Party reactionaries. As Ellen Willis wrote in *Beginning to See the Light*, "My deepest impulses are optimistic, an attitude that seems to me as spiritually necessary and proper as it is intellectually suspect."

Backstage at a benefit concert, singer-songwriter Harry Chapin said, "If you don't act like there's hope, there *is* no hope." So then, hope is a placebo, and placebos work. But when an old friend told me that the official psychiatric *Diagnostic and Statistical Manual of Mental Disorders* had added "Optimism" to its listings, I'm embarrassed to admit that I believed him, if only for a moment. On the other hand, I relish the irony that when I first met him, he was sixteen and attending my class in "Journalism and Satire: How to Tell the Difference." That's getting increasingly difficult these days.

WHY WAS MICHELLE SHOCKED SHELL-SHOCKED?

"Please do not understand me too quickly."
—André Gide

IS MICHELLE SHOCKED HOMOPHOBIC? In March 2013, the singer-songwriter spouted between musical numbers what appeared to be a fanatical Christian anti-gay rant at Yoshi's nightclub in San Francisco:

> But I was in a prayer meeting yesterday, and you gotta appreciate how scared, how scared, folks on that side of the equation are. I mean, from their vantage point—and I really shouldn't say "their," because it's mine, too— we are nearly at the end of time, and from our vantage point, we're gonna be, uh [*facetiously*], I think maybe Chinese water torture is gonna be the means, the method—[*offhanded, flippantly*] once Prop 8 gets instated, and once preachers are held at gunpoint and forced to

marry [*in a character voice*] the homosexuals. I'm pretty sure that will be the signal for Jesus to come on back.

Audience: [*laughter*] Whaaat?

You just said you wanted reality [*laughs*]. If someone would be so gracious as to please tweet out, "Michelle Shocked just said, from stage, 'God hates faggots' [*laughter*]. Would you do it now?" [*laughter*]

Disappointed fans walked out. Yoshi's manager shut off her microphone, insisted that she leave the stage, and banned her from performing there for life. At least fourteen gigs at other venues were annulled, and her career swirled its way down the drain. So she decided to issue this statement:

I believe in a God who loves everyone, and my faith tells me to do my best to also love everyone. Everyone: gay or straight, stridently gay, self-righteously faithful; left or right, far left, far right; good, bad, or indifferent. That's the law: everyone. I may disagree with someone's most fervently held belief, but I will not hate them. And in this controversy, that means speaking for Christians with opinions I in no way share about homosexuality. Will I endorse them? Never. Will I disavow them? Never. I stand accused of forsaking the LGBT community for a Christianity which is—hear me now—anathema to my understanding of faith. I will no doubt take future flack for saying so. I'm accused of believing that "God hates fags" and that the repeal of Prop 8 will usher in the End Times. Well, if I caused such an absurdity, I am damn sorry.

To be clear: I am not now, nor have I ever been, a member of any so-called faith preaching intolerance of anyone. Again, any-one: straight or gay, believers or not: that's the law. That means upholding my punk rock values in the most evangelical enclaves and, in this case, speaking up for the most fearful of fundamentalists in, well, a San Francisco music hall full of Michelle Shocked fans. As an artist in this time of unbearable culture wars, I understand: this means trouble, and this is neither the first nor last time trouble has come my way. And that's fine by me. I know the fear many in the evangelical com-munity feel about homosexual marriage, as I understand the fear many in the gay commu-nity feel toward the self-appointed faithful. I have and will continue speaking to both. Everything else—Facebook, Twitter, what-ever—is commentary.

At midnight on Friday, June 28—the day after the Supreme Court ruling on same-sex marriage, and the beginning of the San Francisco Gay Pride weekend—Michelle was a guest of Daniel Flessas, host of a weekly radio program,

The Outside World, on listener-sponsored KBOO in Portland, Oregon. The call letters of that station were borrowed from a marijuana strain known as "Berkeley Boo."

Having also been invited to participate in the dialogue, I asked Michelle, "Why did you convert to born-again Christianity?"

"I was making an album in 1991 called *Arkansas Traveler* that had its roots in blackface minstrelsy," she replied. "My fiancé was a journalist, deeply researched on the history of the genre. He suggested we attend a local African-American church to explore the contemporary expressions of the music that had inspired the genre, and it was an easy justification.

"Gospel music, what's not to love? Soulful, passionate pyrotechnics, a choir. But I went one Sunday too often and next thing I knew, my feet were making the altar call. The rest of me decided to join them. I went for the singing but stayed for the song. Originally, I recall thinking, 'You know, this music would be so good if they'd just cut out all that Jesus crap.'"

And then Michelle had a question for me:

"My experience has been that people don't wanna let the truth get in the way of a good story. My question to Paul is, having been the *instigator* [*laughs*] of more controversies than I will manage in my lifetime, the absurdity of this situation often causes me to [*laughs*] ask myself—I'm not exaggerating—'What would Paul do?' Surely, there has to be some hilarity that I have overlooked, because I have tried everything I can come up with to make people laugh and to lighten the situation up. What have I forgotten?"

My response: "I think what you forgot was that audiences don't always know the references, and so when you said, 'God hates faggots,' they might not have known that the reactionary Reverend Fred Phelps had said 'God hates fags' and *meant* it, and therefore they assumed that you were saying it as representing *your* belief when you were really, as I understood it, parodying the hatred that Phelps exuded. I mean risk-taking is risky business."

Daniel (host): "But you didn't always explain everything to everyone, did you, Paul?"

"No. When I published satire, I wouldn't label it as satire any more than Jonathan Swift's *Modest Proposal*. He didn't say, 'I'm only kidding, folks, I really don't mean that Irish babies should be eaten by the British in order to simultaneously solve the overpopulation and starvation problems.' And I didn't want to deprive readers of the pleasure of deriving for themselves whether something was literally true or a metaphorical extension of the truth.

"There was a singer named Tonio K. I was invited at the last minute to open for him at the Roxy Theater in L.A.—Harry Shearer was supposed to do it, but he couldn't—and I had never heard of Tonio K. This was at a time when there were all those TV evangelicals—Oral Roberts and Jimmy Swaggart and Jim Bakker—and they were involved in one sex scandal after another, and so I did some material about that. But the audience didn't laugh, and I couldn't figure out why.

"Only later, a review in the *L.A. Times* concluded that I was obviously not aware that Tonio K. was a born-again Christian singer, and that his audience was filled with born-again Christian fans. So I felt relieved, because it was funny material, but humor is totally subjective, and I think that's what Michelle got caught in. The gay community has been so mistreated by people who actually *do* express hostility toward them, it suddenly landed Michelle in that category."

Michelle: "Paul, can I hold your feet to the fire? As the original Zen Bastard, you did not provoke for the sake of provoking, you would never ridicule an audience simply to express some sense of smug superiority. There was always a point and a purpose to the endeavor, and so I would like to submit to you that my efforts were to confound an audience that has grown so self-righteous that they needed a little prick, they needed a little poking. What was that Abbie Hoffman quote? 'Sacred cows make the tastiest hamburger.' I gave them a little taste of the medicine, and they did not like it, not one bit, no sir.

"I am reflecting back that your sensibility was not that of a provocateur, but always of one that would inspire people to think, and my experience with this is that they had grown so entrenched in their dogma that, rather than think, rather than rush to curiosity, I was subjected to a rush to judgment, and I cannot think of anyone that I would like to give more tribute to inspiring [*laughs*] my instigation than you. I'm blaming you for all this, Paul [*laughs*]."

"Yeah, right—I'm the little prick that you referred to."

Michelle confirmed that she would be at the Gay Pride celebration on Sunday morning, "but I will be part of the contingent that is making a statement that San Francisco is proud of Bradley Manning for pursuing his duties as a whistle-blower in revealing secrets that the government would rather not listen to. And we're basically just all gonna raise points that San Francisco Pride leadership rejected the election by all of the former SF Pride grand marshals to name Bradley [now Chelsea] Manning as this year's grand marshal in favor of allowing their sponsors, their military and their corporate sponsors, to dictate the conscience of a community they claim to speak on behalf of, and I would love to be in that great number, marching, proud of a gay soldier who has the interest of everyone in this country above the interests of a few in this country."

On Monday, I e-mailed her and asked how that event went.

"The Bradley Manning contingent in the SF Pride parade was a feisty attempt to put context to the Yoshi's fracas," she replied. "My story, the one I'm sticking to, is that it was a laugh riot, a second line of soul in the middle of a privilege parade. The truth is that I saw and heard countless reasons why any spirit of passionate resistance that once existed has left the disco long ago. It now resembles a Bourbon Street Mardi Gras without King Zulu. Show us yer tits! It's the Rose Parade, and the corporate sponsors write the script. Even the Manning contingent played to the half empty grandstand like dutiful dissidents. The *Star-Spangled Burqa* [an American flag covering her head and body] was a hit, waiting for the photographic/video evidence to appear. So far so censored. I've got this nifty little shot occupying Google at the parade."

And so, returning back to that night at Yoshi's, was Michelle homophobic? Here's an analogy. In 1952, there was a French-and-Italian film, *Seven Deadly Sins*, consisting of seven vignettes, one for each sin—greed, lust, avarice, pride, Dopey, Sneezy, Bashful—and at the end of the seventh sin, the narrator told us that we were going to see the *eighth* sin.

On the screen were all those images that we had been conditioned to associate with the intimations of sin—sailors, hookers, an opium den—and then the narrator explained that the eighth sin was *the desire to see* sin. The audience groaned with a spontaneity that served only to underscore the narrator's point. Sometimes the ultimate target of satire should be its own audience.

OTHER BOOKS BY PAUL KRASSNER

AUTHOR BIO

PAUL KRASSNER PUBLISHED *The Realist* (1958–2001), but when *People* magazine labeled him "father of the underground press," he immediately demanded a paternity test. And when *Life* magazine published a favorable article about him, the FBI sent a poison-pen letter to the editor calling Krassner "a raving, unconfined nut." "The FBI was right," George Carlin responded. "This man is dangerous—and funny, and necessary." While abortion was illegal, Krassner ran an underground referral service, and as an antiwar activist, he became a cofounder of the Yippies (Youth International Party).

Krassner's one-person show won an award from the *L.A. Weekly*. He received an ACLU Uppie (Upton Sinclair) Award for dedication to freedom of expression. At the Cannabis Cup in Amsterdam, he was inducted into the Counterculture Hall of Fame—"my ambition," he claims, "since I was three years old." He won a *Playboy* Award for satire and a Feminist Party Media Workshop Award for journalism. And in 2010 the Oakland branch of the writers' organization PEN honored him with their Lifetime Achievement Award. "I'm very happy to receive this award," he concluded in his acceptance speech, "and even happier that it wasn't posthumous."

FRIENDS OF

These are indisputably momentous times—the financial system is melting down globally and the Empire is stumbling. Now more than ever there is a vital need for radical ideas.

In the six years since its founding—and on a mere shoestring—PM Press has risen to the formidable challenge of publishing and distributing knowledge and entertainment for the struggles ahead. With over 250 releases to date, we have published an impressive and stimulating array of literature, art, music, politics, and culture. Using every available medium, we've succeeded in connecting those hungry for ideas and information to those putting them into practice.

Friends of PM allows you to directly help impact, amplify, and revitalize the discourse and actions of radical writers, filmmakers, and artists. It provides us with a stable foundation from which we can build upon our early successes and provides a much-needed subsidy for the materials that can't necessarily pay their own way. You can help make that happen—and receive every new title automatically delivered to your door once a month—by joining as a Friend of PM Press. And, we'll throw in a free T-shirt when you sign up.

Here are your options:
- $30 a month: Get all books and pamphlets plus 50% discount on all webstore purchases
- $40 a month: Get all PM Press releases (including CDs and DVDs) plus 50% discount on all webstore purchases
- $100 a month: Superstar—Everything plus PM merchandise, free downloads, and 50% discount on all webstore purchases

For those who can't afford $30 or more a month, we're introducing Sustainer Rates at $15, $10, and $5. Sustainers get a free PM Press T-shirt and a 50% discount on all purchases from our website.

Your Visa or Mastercard will be billed once a month, until you tell us to stop. Or until our efforts succeed in bringing the revolution around. Or the financial meltdown of Capital makes plastic redundant. Whichever comes first.

PM Press was founded at the end of 2007 by a small collection of folks with decades of publishing, media, and organizing experience. PM Press co-conspirators have published and distributed hundreds of books, pamphlets, CDs, and DVDs. Members of PM have founded enduring book fairs, spearheaded victorious tenant organizing campaigns, and worked closely with bookstores, academic conferences, and even rock bands to deliver political and challenging ideas to all walks of life. We're old enough to know what we're doing and young enough to know what's at stake.

We seek to create radical and stimulating fiction and non-fiction books, pamphlets, t-shirts, visual and audio materials to entertain, educate, and inspire you. We aim to distribute these through every available channel with every available technology—whether that means you are seeing anarchist classics at our bookfair stalls; reading our latest vegan cookbook at the café; downloading geeky fiction e-books; or digging new music and timely videos from our website.

PM Press is always on the lookout for talented and skilled volunteers, artists, activists, and writers to work with. If you have a great idea for a project or can contribute in some way, please get in touch.

PM Press
PO Box 23912
Oakland CA 94623
510-658-3906
www.pmpress.org